Peter K

Defector

224

MSYNZ

First published in 2019 by MSYNZ

Defector is dedicated to

Cathy,

Bex and James

DEFECTOR

CHAPTER 1 – MARCH 1993

This had better not be locked, Andy thought in the instant before he crashed, shoulder first, into the solid wooden door. The door burst open; its frame splintering with the hard impact. He stumbled onto the busy Moscow street but managed to quickly regain his balance. Turning swiftly, he sprinted off to his left, away from the Government building from which he'd just sprung.

The sidewalk was wide, well maintained and full of office workers going about their daily grind. Even with an efficient and regular Metro service, when the weather was good, like today, commuters preferred to walk in the fresh air rather than head into the stale air of the underground network deep beneath the city.

He dodged and weaved around slower pedestrians. Some of them stopped and turned towards the sound of raised voices coming from the direction of where Andy had first appeared. With their ordered lives, a man running along the sidewalk was unusual and attracted attention; more so if the man was being chased by people shouting for him to stop and he kept running. The growing commotion made more pedestrians stop to witness the unfolding drama of the chase.

Andy clutched the brown file, marked *'CEKPET'*, firmly in his left hand; after the risks he'd taken this morning absently dropping the file was not an option. He headed towards a road junction with traffic-lights and a pedestrian crossing. As he approached, the crossing man changed from red to green. *Yes!* Slowing immediately to a walk, he was able to hide among the mass of pedestrians crossing all at once and take the chance to catch his breath. He also gained more distance from his pursuers and the curious onlookers.

I'm in the clear, he thought with some relief. Then, only a few meters away, a man wearing a tan-colored suit and chocolate brown tie, started yelling and pointing at him. His mind spun. *What the hell!* Running again he could hear the police whistles of the chasers behind him but didn't attempt to check how much distance he'd put between them. In the distance came the unmistakable sound of police sirens; he felt the net closing in on him. His heart pounded rapidly, his mind willing him to move faster and push through the pain. His legs pumped hard, carrying him away from the chasing pack, *I need to go to the gym more*, he thought!

At the next corner he dodged right to avoid a child holding tightly on to her carer's hand and collided with an older woman carrying a large handbag sending her sprawling onto the sidewalk. "Idiot!" the woman shouted in anger as passers-by stopped to see what had happened. Some simply stared at her; others at Andy. He didn't stop and help, he needed to get clear of the area, so he ran without any attempt to apologise; Russian cries of, "Oi! Oi!" and "Stop!", followed him as he fled.

The sound of police whistles seemed to grow closer. Andy glanced quickly behind to check if any 'have a go' heroes were pursuing him; there weren't any. He found the Metro entrance at the next corner and ran down the steps two at a time whilst he stripped off his jacket, rolled it into a small ball and clutched it under his left arm as his left hand still held the file tightly.

As he reached the bottom of the stairs he joined an orderly flow of commuters moving towards the automatic access gates leading to the platforms. He made for the furthest gate and slowed with the queue, then quickly switched to join the file of commuters heading for the exit on the opposite side of the street.

Noticing a small group of young men of a similar age to himself he casually moved over to join them as they walked up the steps into the bright daylight. He turned his head towards one of the group and nodded giving the impression, to anyone watching from a distance, that he was part of their group.

The group turned right out of the Metro and headed in the direction of the woman he'd sent flying moments earlier. *This isn't good*, he thought. Even on the other side of the busy road with plenty of people around him there was still a chance she would look up and see him. Luck was on his side as she seemed intent on continuing her commute and didn't look in his direction. He felt safe, for now, so continued moving with the general flow of pedestrians.

He edged towards the side of the sidewalk closest to the store fronts. Stepping through the open door of a small bakery he stopped, looked at the owner behind the counter and gave the kind of nonchalant shrug that said he'd forgotten why he'd entered. He turned and left stepping back onto the sidewalk, only this time heading towards his extraction point.

He became conscious that, unlike the people around him, beads of sweat poured down his forehead and his armpits were heavily sweat-stained. He approached the corner where he exited the Metro and felt safer. *Almost there*, he told himself, *don't make any sudden moves to draw attention.*

Then, a voice, shouted, "Police! Police!" Andy swung round to locate the owner. It was the man in the tan-colored suit standing at the top of the Metro steps only meters away. Making a spilt second decision he rushed towards the man. The man's eyes widened with a look of surprise as Andy easily covered the short distance and then threw a punch which connected hard to the man's jaw. The man's eyes lost focus and he tumbled backwards down the Metro stairs; he made no attempt to break his fall and landed in an untidy heap at the bottom of the steps.

A policeman appeared and approached the unconscious man. Andy realised that he'd paused too long as the policeman looked up and locked eyes with him. "Stop! Police!" the policeman shouted, reaching for his holstered pistol as he moved towards the steps. *No way!* Andy thought as he took off at speed.

He'd memorised the plan. He needed to make it to the end of the next block, turn right and the yellow Lada Riva would be waiting for him, engine running, the driver ready to put his foot down as soon as Andy was inside. *I can be there in one minute as long as I don't body-check anyone else or get shot!* The sound of a police whistle screeched from the Metro entrance and spurred him on faster.

As he reached the end of the block he glanced backwards. He saw at least a dozen police officers closing in on him from both sides of the sidewalk. Traffic horns blared loudly in protest as the police forced cars to brake hard so they could get across the road. He had about minute lead, at most, on the chasing posse. Andy turned the corner and made ready to snatch open the door to the Lada and then … he came to an abrupt halt.

"What the fuck?" Andy cursed as a wave of panic washed over him and his eyes searched frantically for his way out, "Where the hell is he?"

CHAPTER 2

With less than thirty seconds before the police would be turning the corner and joining him there was no time to stand still; he had to improvise. He saw an old grey Volvo parked two bays along with a driver and its engine running. *Have they changed the extraction car without telling me?* he asked himself, *no time to check, I'll just have to act and ask questions later!* He opened the passenger door and jumped in beside the driver.

"What the ...?" the driver protested.

This wasn't his driver, clearly a civilian, and a surprised one at that; his extraction was now officially screwed. Safe in the knowledge that most people in Russia had something to hide gave him an angle to work with: "Go! Go! Go! They're coming for you!" Andy screamed in Russian.

The driver looked panicked and confused: "Get out of my car!" he protested.

"I'm here to warn you, but I'm late. They're here. Move! Now!" The driver still wasn't responding. "They knew you'd be here. It's a set-up. Make your mind up. Stay here and get robbed and beaten or escape. Now!" Andy watched as the driver quickly worked through his options. His own heart raced as precious seconds had been eaten up since turning the corner but, to Andy's relief, the driver decided not to argue further, put the car in gear and pulled out into the busy traffic; moments later they were invisible among the other vehicles.

Andy leaned forward and looked in the Volvo's side mirror to catch the street scene behind them. Four police officers had just turned the corner and were now having a discussion. *That was a bit too close for comfort*, he thought as he continued to observe. One officer stepped away and talked into his radio while the other three worked their way along the line of cars towards the Volvo: two officers ran along the sidewalk; the third ran between the lanes of slow-moving vehicles. They glanced into each vehicle making split-second decisions on whether they'd found their quarry before moving on to the next. Andy caught a glimpse of their drawn sidearms.

His attention to the rear was distracted by more movement, this time at junction they were approaching. He could see about a dozen uniformed police officers forming a line and starting to move towards them. The net was quickly closing in on him.

"Get us out of here!" Andy shouted as he slammed his open palm on the grey plastic trim of the Volvo's dashboard: "It's the police too!" he had no idea of the meaning of what he said but it sounded good.

"I'm stuck in traffic or are you blind?" the driver spat back.

The traffic moved towards the junction and closer to the approaching line of police, Andy saw a side road on the right and, hoping it wasn't a dead end, shouted: "Right! Turn right!" The Volvo took the turn a bit too quickly, as when Andy leaned forward to look in the mirror, one of the officers was pointing frantically towards them. Two officers gave chase but were not fast enough to catch up with the Volvo as its driver eased up the gears. Realising they were falling behind, one of the officers stopped, raised his pistol and quickly squeezed off four rounds.

At the sound of the gunshots Andy instinctively ducked down. He knew the thin metal skin of the car would offer no protection from the lethal projectiles. One clearly hit its target but Andy had no way of knowing where, the driver didn't seem to notice; he was focused on getting as far away as possible without being shot or arrested or both!

A white box van, with loud thumping rock music bellowing out of its windows, appeared behind the Volvo shielding it but blocking Andy's view of the chase. *Shit!* he cursed. The police sirens seemed to be growing louder and, although Andy hadn't caught sight of any police vehicles yet, he knew they wouldn't be far away. "Take the next right!" Andy ordered.

The driver took the turn followed by the white van which stayed pinned to their bumper. After a few more turns, left and right, they lost the white van and Andy instructed the driver to turn back onto the main road. They were now a safe distance from the intersection and would avoid detection.

They kept moving with the flow of the traffic and were soon clear of the immediate area; Andy listened to the police sirens fading as they continued to drive further away. "What the hell happened back there?" the driver demanded. Andy now had the luxury of time to think of a reasonable story within the realms of truth without giving too much away for both their protection.

"Um, a bit of a misunderstanding … a case of mistaken identity … better to get away and sort it out later."

The driver nodded, he understood the need to be a cagey and didn't push Andy to elaborate. They drove in silence for a few minutes before the driver introduced himself, "Vladimir Martirossian."

"Andy Flint. Thanks for getting us out of there."

"I went to get cash from the bank. I'd best get back to my office as I can't go to the bank with all the police out there now looking for my car."

"Don't worry. You'll be fine." Andy said giving the driver a once over. Like Andy, he was in his early twenties; unlike Andy, Vladimir had a shaven head and old bruising on his neck and around his eyes where he'd taken a beating. Vladimir noticed Andy looking at him instead of the road ahead.

"What are you looking at?"

"Just wanted to see who helped me out. I don't want to forget a friendly face." Andy could feel the atmosphere change and tension radiate from Vladimir; they drove in silence for the rest of their journey. Andy used the time to put on his jacket and stuff the file inside before zipping up his jacket to conceal it from immediate prying eyes.

The car slowed as it approached a six-story concrete apartment block. Vladimir drove into a run-down garage through open grey metal doors located to the right-side of the apartment block. Vladimir stopped and quickly got out of the car making his way around the rear of the vehicle to close the doors. As he closed the first door he glanced back and stopped.

"What the hell?" Vladimir cursed, "Look what you've done to my car!"

Andy joined Vladimir to survey the damage and couldn't miss the large bullet hole in the rear tailgate. The bullet had made a mess of the back seat and exited through the floor between the two front seats. "It's not too bad. You can still drive it," Andy said optimistically.

"If I take this to a garage they'll call the police," Vladimir groaned and added, "even in Moscow a bullet hole in your car would raise questions."

"Don't take it to a garage, I'll see what I can do," Andy said hoping to defuse Vladimir's anger, "I know some people who can help." He didn't, but at this moment in time, a small white lie was the least of his problems. He was unsure of his location or the person standing next to him; a wrong move could put him in a whole heap of trouble so he needed to keep the driver sweet and not add fuel to his anger. Vladimir paced up and down for a moment with both hands on his head.

"My day isn't going well. I needed the money from the bank. Now I have no money, a bullet hole in my car and the police are out there searching for it!" he exclaimed while wafting his right hand in the general direction of the city. Once they were both outside the garage Vladimir finished closing up and locked the doors. Turning to Andy he said, "Come up to my office. I think we both need a stiff drink."

Andy nodded and followed Vladimir to the communal entrance of the apartment block where he stopped and turned to face Andy. "My friends call me Vladim," he said, offering his hand for Andy to shake. Andy didn't hesitate and the two men exchanged a warm handshake. In the short time they'd been acquainted they'd been through an interesting introduction to their 'friendship'. Andy relaxed a little, but not too much as he knew it would be a mistake to drop his guard. They entered the block and made their way up the chipped concrete stairs to the third floor. They continued along a drab corridor with reinforced steel doors off to the right. Eventually Vladim stopped at a dark-green steel door.

Andy noticed the door was slightly ajar and, with Vladim emitting a deep sign as he pushed the door fully open, his level of alertness was raised. He followed Vladim inside preparing to react to what was on the other side of the door. *I could do without more surprises today*. He thought.

The entrance hall had been fitted out as a rather cramped reception area. Just off from the reception area, Andy saw what appeared to be a meeting room and watched as Vladim step through its entrance. Andy peered in and saw four leather-jacketed men sitting around a large wooden table. They looked like the local hoods. A muscle-bound bald man with a long grey beard spoke first.

"Mr Popov is waiting for you in your office."

Vladim abruptly turned on his heels out of the room, almost colliding with Andy, and walked round the corner, through a large working area, where there were rows of desks stacked with computers, boxes and bulky monitors, towards an office on the far side of the room. The office door was wide open and Vladim walked purposefully inside.

Behind a cluttered desk sat a small fat man wearing a dark-blue suit with a dark-green shirt and light-blue tie; his feet elevated and resting on the desktop. The man remained seated when Vladim entered, his hand-stitched Italian shoes didn't move from the desk. *I don't like you already*. Thought Andy … then the man started to talk.

"Martirossian, you have my money?"

"No Max, there was a …"

Before he could say more the fat man sat up and slapped his hand hard on the desk.

"Mr Popov to you!"

"I'm sorry, Mr Popov, I had a problem at the bank. There was an incident or something and I couldn't get the money. There were police everywhere and I had to leave."

"Has your lover boy here got any money?" Popov pointed with his stubby index finger towards Andy.

Andy regretted not following the advice he'd been given to carry a firearm on the operation as at this moment he would have felt a lot happier if his right hand was caressing the butt of his favored semi-automatic. Instead Andy looked on apologetic as Popov slowly looked him up and down.

"I thought not."

A long silence followed as Popov considered his options.

"I'll give you twenty-four hours … but it will cost you another five hundred." Vladim took a sharp intake of breath in shock at the number just added to his debt. "If you don't pay up, I'll just have to start breaking things, maybe, your lover boy's legs first," Popov pointed at Andy, "then your arms and, finally, your business. You understand?"

What the hell have I walked into?

Popov stood up and headed for the door. As he walked past Vladim he paused and slapped Vladim gently on the left cheek. "Don't force me to let Ivan and his boys loose on you. They're in need of a good workout … all that pent-up aggression waiting to be released."

Popov continued on his way with Vladim and Andy following. The four thugs loitered in the reception area, the cramped space now even smaller than it had appeared moments earlier. Popov exited through the open entrance way and once in the corridor he called out.

"Twenty-four hours …"

CHAPTER 3

"You finished that quickly," Grant Manchester said to Andy, "here, have another." Grant was Head of Station and Andy's ultimate boss in Russia. He had a reputation for being a tough taskmaster, though today, Grant had been all smiles and back slapping as he handed Andy another chilled beer from the refrigerator. "Some stunt you pulled this morning."

"Thank you, sir."

"The file you lifted is a treasure trove of new information for us. We now know for certain what the Politburo is thinking about the Constitutional referendum in two weeks, and how little support Yeltsin actually has within his own cabinet. It will keep our analysts busy for months; the intelligence reports it contained gives us the opportunity to disrupt several KGB operations on US soil and in Germany."

Manchester will be the toast of Langley. It'll look good on his annual review, Andy thought. "I'm surprised they didn't take more care of their Politburo files, if I'd not been disturbed I could have taken the lot."

Manchester gently held Andy's right arm and led him out of earshot from his co-workers. "I expect great things from you, son. I hope you aren't one of those one hit wonders. If you are, I'll not hesitate in giving you a poor performance review and have you shipped home."

Andy wasn't expecting this and wasn't sure how to respond, "I won't let you down, sir." Were the only words he could find. Manchester patted Andy on the shoulder, "I know you won't." Manchester led him back to the main group of celebrating intelligence staff. They went their separate ways to different groups as the party atmosphere continued with staff taking the opportunity to relax and share a few stories.

Andy had just started his third beer and was deep in conversation with one of the junior administrators when the room fell unexpectedly quiet. He looked around and saw a small group clustered in a huddle. Someone lay on the floor. He couldn't make out who it was, but he did recognise Frank Brown from the Marine Corps kneeling over the person and applying chest compressions.

"Someone call Doc!" Brown shouted. Andy moved closer to see who had collapsed and reeled in shock when he saw Grant Manchester on the floor, his face a pale grey color. Brown blew air into his chest; then carried on with the compressions. A few minutes later, the group parted as Doc Hall, the Embassy's Medic known to all as 'Doc', approached the casualty.

"Okay folks. You've all seen enough. Clear out of here while Frank and I deal with this," Doc said calmly. Doc with his battered leather medical bag knelt next to Brown and asked for a quick update. Andy watched as he checked Manchester's pulse. Doc's face showed only concern as he bit onto his lower lip and made a call. "Keep going," he instructed Brown.

Doc reached into his bag and with two hands produced a portable defibrillator which he placed on the floor. He quickly ripped Manchester's shirt open, peeled the backing off the conductive pads and attached them, connected the lead from the pads into the defibrillator and pressed the large green on button. An automated voice took over and after a few seconds recommended applying a shock. "Stand Clear!" Doc shouted. After checking all was clear he pressed the red button and the defibrillator sounded three short beeps followed by a long one as it applied a shock to Manchester's chest.

Time seemed to stop as they waited for the machine to re-analyse Manchester's heart rhythm. A few seconds later the automated voice instructed Doc and Grant to continue CPR.

Andy made his way out of the room as Doc took over from Brown in giving chest compressions. Although he couldn't see what was happening, he could hear their efforts as they fought to keep Manchester alive. Two minutes later he heard Doc shout, "Stand Clear", followed by the machine's short beeps as it shocked Manchester again. He was relieved when he heard Doc announce: "There's a faint pulse. He's breathing. We've got him back."

The room cleared leaving Doc and Grant looking after Manchester. With the atmosphere now sombre, the celebration had fizzled out. Apart from a few people who were concerned about Manchester, the rest of the staff left decided head home earlier than normal. Andy headed out of the Embassy with Tex Striker for their safe house a few blocks away.

Tex and Andy had recently graduated from 'The Farm' together and that was where their similarities ended. Tex was a bear of a man. Just over six four of solid muscle, he'd turned down offers of pro-football to realise his dream of serving his country through the Agency. Together Andy and Tex had been finding their way around Moscow and learning about the field work the Agency conducted in Moscow.

While Andy and Tex got along, they had very different personalities which sometimes grated on Andy. Andy respected other people's personal space; Tex had no concept of personal space … it was all his. Andy tried to keep the volume of his music down or the noise from his television manageable; Tex showed no restraint … he believed sound was meant to travel. While Andy tidied up after himself; Tex was quite happy to leave their small kitchen in a mess for several days before tidying it up … or watching Andy tidy it up. Andy knew where the vacuum cleaner was and how it operated; Tex claimed no knowledge and showed no indication he was inclined to learn. Andy was punctual to the point of being five minutes early; Tex, on the other hand, was consistently late.

But Tex had a great sense of humor and his charisma always lit up the room. He was loud, playful but, more importantly, he was loyal. With the evening still early, the two men stopped at a small bar in a side street for a few drinks before heading using different paths to the safe house. A healthy precautionary measure drilled into them at 'The Farm'.

***

The following morning when Andy arrived at the Embassy, he found a note on his desk asking him to meet with Carrie Roper, Grant's number two. Andy looked around and saw Carrie by the communal coffee percolator and he wandered over to find out what she wanted. She led him into one of the windowless meeting rooms.

"Andrew, you pulled off an amazing coup lifting the Politburo file yesterday."

"Thank you. How's Grant?"

She looked concerned and took her time to figure out what to say. "He's had a heart attack. Frank and Doc were able to revive and stabilise him. They saved his life. We put him on a diplomatic flight as an emergency medivac case to Ramstein Airbase in Germany. They operated on him last night. I'm told it was a bit touch and go a few times, but he's a fighter and pulled through. He'll be out of action for a few months."

"It's good to hear he's going to be okay."

"It is good news, but our work doesn't stop. We have a real-time situation which I need you to deal with in Grant's absence."

Andy was intrigued "I'm listening."

"I'm desk based. I run operations. I'm not a field agent," said Carrie.

"And?"

"We've been contacted by one of our key assets, an FSB Colonel. He wants to meet urgently. Grant had been his regular handler, with no Grant, that's now you."

Carrie slid a brown paper file, marked '*Top Secret*', across the table. "You're meeting him in half an hour, so read quickly; that file doesn't leave this room."

"Before I read the file, what can you tell me about him?"

"The Colonel has been an asset of the Agency for several years. From what I know he's been highly reliable and of great value to us."

"Do you trust him?"

Carrie laughed.

"What do you think? I don't even trust you!"

CHAPTER 4

The Embassy minibus drove to the corner of Znamenka and Mokhovaya Street stopping briefly to give Andy time to get out and close the door. He was immediately among the throng of morning commuters. Andy felt pretty safe in the knowledge he wasn't being followed as he made his way to Borovitskaya Metro Station, only a short distance from the Kremlin.

He descended the steps into the Metro, headed for the barriers and used a Metro token in the turnstile before making his way down to the platform. He was wearing an old grey suit with worn brown shoes; to complete the look he wore thick framed glasses with clear lenses and carried a battered leather briefcase. He easily blended in among the crowd of government workers patiently waiting for the train going north to Otradnoye.

He checked his plastic digital watch at the same moment the station public address system announced the imminent arrival of the next train. To make sure he'd be in the first carriage to leave the station he carefully threaded his way through the crowd of waiting commuters towards the distant end of the platform. The rush of air around him, the electronic hum from the transmission gear and a loud clattering of carriages announced the arrival of the train which moved rapidly along the platform. The piercing metallic squeal from the train's brakes echoed loudly off the curved walls as the train slowed and pulled to a halt a few meters in front of him.

Andy waited while a wall of passengers alighted from the train before he stepped inside the still crowded metal tube. He moved over to the far door, making room for other commuters to get on board and grabbed the hand rail to steady himself. Next to him stood a man wearing a smart, dark grey, three-piece suit, white shirt and dark red tie. He wore thin black leather gloves and held onto the hand rail as the doors to the train closed and the train accelerated out of the station.

"I've not seen leather gloves like those in years. Where did you get them?" Andy asked the suited man.

"I bought them on Oxford Street in London," the man replied.

"Did you get to see the Tate Modern?"

"No. I'm not an art lover. I did go to Saint Paul's; it offers stunning views over London."

This is my guy. He has authenticated correctly. Andy thought.

"What's with the need for the urgent meeting?" Andy asked.

"Where's Grant?" came the reply. The Colonel's English was good.

"He's been taken ill and had to leave the country, that's why I'm here."

"I hope he makes a full recovery, but who are you?"

"Andy Flint, I'm the new kid on the block."

"Nice to meet you Andy. You closely resemble the man in the photos issued after yesterday's theft from the Government archives."

"That's interesting," Andy didn't want to give too much away; he didn't know if anyone was listening.

13

"Yes, we were impressed with his audacity and cunning. He caught the guards asleep on the toilet, so heads will roll," The Colonel chuckled, "I must remember to never underestimate you."

"So why are we here?"

"I must defect to the West within a week."

"What?" as soon as the word left his lips, Andy immediately kicked himself for revealing his surprise.

"There's a new and rising star in the FSB. His name is Oleg Malchik. He wants to make a name for himself and is conducting an aggressive hunt for moles within our Government and its agencies. His searchlight has been cast over me and its beam is starting to focus in."

"How do you know this?"

"Malchik has already taken out two administrators who were working for French intelligence. An SVR agent who took money from the Germans and three diplomats who had been compromised and were working for the British. With those 'wins' on his board, Malchik has been allowed to sharpen his claws."

"And now you believe he's coming after you?"

"Yes. If I'm lucky, I have a week. You need to get me out," The Colonel looked relaxed as he spoke.

"I'm new here. I'll look into it and see what I can do."

"You're a resourceful young man. I don't see the slow wheels of bureaucracy being much of an obstacle to you."

The train slowed as it pulled into Chekhovskaya.

"This is my stop," The Colonel announced, "I'll be on this train at six this evening."

"Okay."

The doors opened and just before The Colonel stepped off the train, he turned to face Andy: "If you don't move quickly it will be the firing squad for me." The Colonel turned and joined the crowd exiting onto the platform. The doors closed and the train moved on, Andy glanced back but The Colonel had already disappeared from view.

CHAPTER 5

With Vladim's office three blocks from the Metro station, Andy had planned his route back to the Embassy taking in a small detour. He made his way to the front door and rang the bell. After a long wait, Vladim opened the door. He didn't look that pleased to see Andy, "Don't just stand there. Come in. Quick!"

Vladim opened the door just wide enough for Andy to push past into the reception area where an assortment of broken wood that was once office furniture together with other debris which littered the floor. Vladim led Andy through the workshop, almost everything there was broken too. A few members of staff were picking up the pieces in an attempt to bring some order to the chaos. In Vladim's office large graffiti, sprayed on the wall in black paint read simply: 'Get my money!'

"Why would Popov do this to you when you were going to pay him?"

"He wants to make my life difficult so I can't pay. If I can't pay, he then takes a lucrative share of my business, so I have him earning from my profits too."

The two men sat and faced each other at the table.

"How did you get into this mess?"

"As soon as we moved into these offices we were approached by Popov and his thugs. Ivan was the one who spoke to me yesterday ... he's named after "Ivan the Terrible" for good reason! The deal was to either pay his weekly protection money or have staff beaten, goods damaged and customers intimidated."

"What did you do?"

"What do you think? I paid. Initially the amounts were small, but the numbers soon grew. I saw a pattern emerge from the businesses around me. They too had their local taxation increased until the only way they could clear their debt was to make Popov a business partner. That's why my stock and my office have been trashed; he wants me on my knees."

"Have you been to the police?"

Vladim laughed. "You're new to this aren't you? I pay Popov ... he pays the police. You see my problem? The police won't help me."

Andy reached into his jacket and removed a stack of hundred dollar bills: "I can give you two thousand dollars for helping me out of my spot of bother yesterday."

With hungry eyes Vladim looked at the money: "That will go a long way to paying off Popov."

Andy realised that the two thousand dollars he'd brought with him wouldn't cover the debt so he added, "I'm waiting for the compensation to come through from Finance so you can repair your car. The payment will be generous as we also want to buy your silence."

Vladim smiled: "Thanks!" and quickly tucked the money inside his jacket pocket.

The guy looks genuinely happy, Andy thought. "Do you want help clearing up?" Andy asked.

"No. I've got plenty of idle hands who are clearing up or making deliveries. I need to go to the bank to draw more cash and pay Popov in full. If you can get me a few thousand dollars more, I'd be grateful and I'd forget that you were carrying that file."

Andy smiled and carefully threaded his way through the debris as he headed for the exit. Vladim stayed a few paces behind as he issued instructions and words of encouragement to his staff.

Outside the apartment block as they stepped onto the sidewalk, Andy spotted two men in leather jackets positioned across the road. They'd been smoking while watching the stairs and on seeing Vladim, quickly discarded their cigarettes into the gutter and started to follow them. Andy headed for the Metro with Vladim at his side.

"You're not driving?"

"At this time of day, with that large bullet hole, I think my car might attract unwanted attention."

"You may have a point."

The two men trailing just behind stayed together on the opposite side of the street. After two blocks, a black BMW with frosted glass drove slowly past and pulled in. *Now what do you want?* Andy muttered to himself. Their two followers made their move to cross the street. "Run!" Andy shouted, "head for the alleyway on the right."

Vladim had a good running technique and already had two metres on Andy by the time they reached the narrow alleyway. Andy turned and saw the two thugs running after them. They were not fit nor built for running and had fallen behind. As he turned into the alleyway he glanced back at the BMW. Popov was now stood with two more thugs and looked unimpressed at the efforts of his two runners who had slowed down to walking pace. Andy pushed harder to catch Vladim and by the time they reached the exit to the alleyway he could have touched him. The Beretta in its shoulder holster had restricted his arm swing, though he was still happy with his effort to have caught Vladim.

"Head for the Metro!" he managed to get out. Vladim turned left and took the steps two at a time down into the Metro. Andy saw the BMW speeding towards them as he descended the steps. He watched as Vladim didn't slow, easily clearing the entry barrier, but Andy didn't feel he would make it so effortlessly, so he stopped and hurriedly fed a token into the slot. As the barrier opened he sprinted after Vladim.

Andy reached the platform as a Metro train entered the station and started to slow down. Vladim had stopped and looked around anxiously. Andy joined him as the train doors opened. They stepped inside together with a large school group and their teachers. The teenage girls were dressed in their smart blue uniforms which sported a strip of red tartan across the pockets and around the cuffs, and talked excitedly among themselves.

Andy positioned himself behind two of the teachers to conceal himself from anyone looking into the train from the platform. The doors closed and moments later, the train started to accelerate out of the station. Andy looked back down the platform at the faces waiting for the next train. He spotted Popov with Ivan and three of his thugs, and he could see they were scanning the sea of faces looking for Vladim. Seconds later the train entered the darkness of tunnel.

They took two stops before they left the train.

"Andy, this is where we say, goodbye, I need to get to the bank as I want to avoid any more 'extras' on my debt."

"I'll come back to your office when I have some extra cash."

"Great, I'll see you then," Vladim replied.

The two men shook hands and headed for different exits. Andy paused, turned and watched Vladim disappear into the crowd before he continued on his way, not spotting the two women, a discreet distance behind, following him as he exited.

***

Carrie Roper looked alarmed as Andy delivered the news that one of their prime assets wanted out, and quickly. "I'm sure we'll take him … it's just the timescales … defections take months of detailed planning and multiple layers of sign-off before we get the green light."

"So, you don't believe he'll be out of Russia in a week?" Andy asked.

"In a week? We won't get an answer on whether he'd be welcome Stateside in a month!" Carrie tried to look upbeat. "I'm sure we'll take him," she repeated, "he's been a valuable asset for years."

"Do I need to speak to anyone?" Andy asked.

"No. Leave it with me. I've got a good working relationship with Langley. I'll raise it with the Assistant Director. He'll raise it with State and check in with The White House." Carrie smiled; one of those false *'smiling for no reason'* smiles. Her eyes fixed on the door behind him, then flicked briefly back to Andy as she spoke, "Andrew, I'm sure you've got lots to be getting along with," she looked back towards the door.

Meeting's over, Andy thought. "I need to check in with Finance and put a claim in for the damage made to the civilian's car. I don't want him making trouble for me."

"Yes, Yes, Yes, make sure you fill in the correct form. It's the J101F. Bring it to me and I'll sign it."

"Thanks." Andy turned and left the room. Carrie remained behind, her fixed smile still in place.

He headed up to the third floor where the small finance team was located. Up until today he'd never filed a claim for anything, not even a Metro ticket. Now he'd be asking for ten thousand dollars in cash. Andy pressed the door bell and, after a short delay, they 'buzzed' him in through the heavily reinforced door. Following a quick conversation with one of the admin staff he walked out with two J101F's. The second just in case he made an expected mistake on the first, which they told him was common for most newbies. Andy didn't think he'd need it but took it anyway; he didn't want to spend more time than necessary in the sterile environment as everything had its place, even the paperclips!

Back at his desk Andy got to work on the finance form. He sat and thought for a few moments about the question *'Reason for your claim'*. Then wrote:

> 'During the extraction phase of a covert operation, the Russian Authorities attempted to apprehend me. Due to the fluidity of the situation, and in order to escape imminent capture, I commandeered a civilian vehicle. The driver of the vehicle complied with my instructions to leave the area. The Russian Authorities fired at the vehicle causing damage to the exterior, interior and the owners property. The owner was in the process of delivering computer supplies and the bullets damaged much of his stock. The claim is to pay for repairs to the vehicle, to compensate for the replacement stock and to buy his silence.'

The damaged computer supplies were a small white lie. True, stock had been damaged, but the location was Vladim's office and not his car.

Tex Striker appeared with a coffee in hand and a large goofy smile across his face, "Hey buddy. What are you doing there?" he asked.

"Paperwork. Making an expense claim."

"Oh."

Andy knew Tex wasn't one for paperwork.

"You want me to grab you a coffee?"

"No. I'm nearly done."

"Hey … um … thanks for not mentioning I was late and didn't park at the pick-up point."

"I've got your back. You've got mine."

"Do you want me to check it? A fresh pair of eyes?" He offered as he gestured towards the form with his coffee mug. Andy felt it wouldn't hurt. With the form completed he slid it across to Tex who studied it for only a few seconds, before he took a step back, clicked the fingers on his right hand and pointed with his index finger at the form. "There it is!" he said with a high degree of satisfaction.

"Go on?" Andy looked at the form.

"You put today's date. The incident with the car was yesterday, right?" Andy slapped his forehead with the palm of his hand. Tex moved forward and slid the form back. Andy started to complete the second form, while Tex returned to his own desk.

With the form correctly completed, Andy headed over to Carrie's office to get it signed. Through her open door he could hear Carrie's raised voice. Andy paused, waiting for an opportune moment to present his claim.

"Greg. Come on. Cut us some slack … The Colonel wouldn't make the request if he didn't need to … you knew about the Germans and the Brits losing their assets before I told you. So you know The Colonel is at risk …"

Andy decided he'd wait and continue to listen.

"You're telling me he can't surrender to the Embassy or Consulate in Russia … can he make his own way out of the country?" Carrie sounded perplexed. "Can he then surrender? … What? … Not even to a former Communist Country like Poland? Let me get this straight, he can defect as long as we don't help him leave Russia and he hands himself over to one of our missions in the West, and 'West' doesn't mean a former Soviet satellite country? Okay … thanks Greg … Yes? …Flint? … I'll pass on your comments regarding his recent assignment … Talk soon … Bye."

Andy didn't need to work out what had been discussed. He'd been trained to join the dots. He slowly counted to five before knocking on the door.

"Come in!" Carrie shouted.

Andy entered. The office was pretty standard for a mid-level manager at the Agency. The only trace of personalisation was a wooden photo frame containing a photo of a man and two young girls. Andy assumed them to be of her husband and kids.

"You got that J101F for me to sign?" Andy handed the form to her which she read quickly, "You believe ten thousand will cover repairs to his car, the loss of his stock and buy his silence?" She tapped the form where he'd indicated the value of the claim.

"Yes."

"Here's what I'm going to do. I'm amending your claim to twenty thousand. You take Tex with you and I want Tex to take photos of you handing the money over to ..." She quickly found the name on the form, "... Vladimir Martirossian ... that way if he thinks he can turn you in, you've got him by the balls."

"Okay."

Carrie amended the form, initialled the change, signed and dated it. She handed the form back to Andy. "Take it to finance and they'll give you the funds. Oh ... about The Colonel, Langley support the defection, however, he has to make his way to a friendly Western country. He can't make the move in a former Soviet Satellite country and he's got to do it on his own."

Andy knew not to argue. Carrie's hands had been tied by Greg.

"Okay. I'll let The Colonel know tonight."

"Good. Oh, one more thing, the Assistant Director was impressed with yesterday's operation and the data we gathered from the document. You certainly got the attention of the people upstairs. Keep up the good work Andrew," she smiled.

Andy smiled in return and left the office making his way back to Finance.

CHAPTER 6

Right on time, he thought as he stepped onto the waiting train. The Colonel cut a distinguished figure among the commuters making him easy to spot. Andy held back for a few moments as he studied the faces around The Colonel before he approached. Andy stood next to The Colonel and faced away as he initiated the contact authentication process.

"I've not seen leather gloves like those in years. Where did you get them?"

"I bought them on Oxford Street in London," came the reply.

So far so good. "Did you get to see the Tate Modern?"

"Yes. I went there with my friends."

This is wrong. He's being tailed. Why didn't I spot them? Andy chastised himself before continuing with the authentication. "Do your friends live near you?"

"Yes. Very near, almost on top of me. You will meet them if you stick around long enough."

"Okay. Let's keep this short. The party for your brother is all good with the party planners. Your brother just needs to make his own way to their main office in Amsterdam."

"Can you help distract him to make it a big surprise when he finds out?"

"I'll work on that for you."

"Good, meet me tomorrow night at ten in Gorky Park, south entrance, off Titovsky. I'll be taking my regular walk with my neighbour's dog."

Andy didn't reply. He moved away from The Colonel. Moments later the train entered the next station and slowed to a stop at the platform. When the doors opened, he avoided the natural impulse to turn and look back, instead he focussed on getting out of the Metro and spotting any tails he'd picked up; if there were any he'd be able to lose them quickly enough.

He made his way along the busy platform and buried himself among the crowd. He cut into one of the exits keeping close to the right wall, the passenger tunnel made a right and then left. Andy switched his position so he now hugged the left wall. On his left, another exit from the platform, had disgorged more commuters into the tunnel. Andy ducked down slightly and spun left walking close to the right wall again, nimbly dodging the wave of exiting commuters. With a final left turn, he found himself back on the platform, where, less than a minute or so earlier, he'd alighted from the train.

The Colonel's train had gone and the platform started to steadily fill with commuters getting ready to catch the next train. *Do I stay for the next train and risk being caught or do I leave and risk being caught as I walk into their net?* Andy thought as he considered his next move. He hadn't picked up anyone following him so he was confident he'd either lost them or he wasn't the target and The Colonel was in a heap of trouble.

His realised he was breathing rapidly and could feel his heart racing as if it might burst out from his chest. An announcement over the station PA system told the gathering commuters the next train would be arriving in two minutes. *Stay. Go. Stay. Go.* He was irritated that he was being so indecisive.

Andy took a moment to calm his breathing while he looked around. He realised he couldn't go anywhere as he'd now be easy to spot if he decided to leave; a lone commuter leaving the platform in between train arrivals would definitely draw attention. Andy moved along the platform to join a small cluster of men waiting for their ride home.

A man further down the platform caught Andy's attention. Andy recalled the man had been on the train when he had met The Colonel. The man wore a long grey coat and had been standing next to a younger man who wore a black leather jacket and sported a 'Freddie Mercury' style moustache. To Andy it looked like the two men were travelling together.

Now 'Grey Coat' was walking in Andy's direction. That in itself wasn't suspicious but from where he was positioned Andy could see he was slowly and deliberately studying each male face. Andy looked away but kept 'Grey Coat' in his peripheral vision. Then he spotted 'Freddie' approaching from the other direction also closely studying each male face. The man's leather jacket couldn't conceal the bulge of a shoulder holster and pistol. Andy realised he was stuck between the two men who he assumed were Russian FSB Agents. *So much for staying put!*

The air pressure in the station changed as a gust of air blew down the platform, followed by a roar as the leading carriage entered the station. Andy watched as the train moved down the platform and started to brake with its wheels emitting a high pitch metallic screech in protest. Andy looked along the platform and saw all the commuters were looking at the slowing train except 'Freddie', his eyes were locked on Andy. *Shit!* Andy quickly looked to his left and, to his dismay, he saw that 'Grey Coat' had also seen him and was working his way through the crowd.

The train came to a halt and almost immediately the doors opened allowing a mass of commuters to spill out of the carriage onto the platform and adding to the already crowded space. Andy stepped onto the train. He saw both 'Grey Coat' and 'Freddie' get onto the train each two carriages down either side of his carriage. Andy remained hidden in the crush and out of the view of his pursuers. No further commuters were leaving or entering the carriage. Andy paused for a moment before rushing for the open doors. As he'd cleared them, the doors closed behind him and he landed on the empty platform.

He watched the train as it accelerated away. 'Freddie' pressed his face against the window, his eyes scanning the platform, when he saw Andy, his mouth contorted with a sneer. Andy turned and moving quickly caught up with the tail end of the exiting commuters.

CHAPTER 7

Exiting the Metro, the warmth from the sun's rays washed over Andy making the decision to walk across the central city to the safe house an easy one. He'd use the safe house as a base where, without interruptions, he could think of a plan for The Colonel.

He walked along Tverskaya Street, then moving with the flow of the other pedestrians, he took the underpass to Mokhovaya Street. His mind was working through the outline of a distraction plan for The Colonel when he walked past four of Popov's thugs who were busy shaking down a stallholder for protection money. The stallholder had to be in her seventies and looked distressed. He could hear her protests as they thumbed through her record collection and demanded free samples of the cheap Vodka she sold.

One of the four stood to one side smoking a cigarette from the corner of his mouth. *Ivan*, Andy thought as he continued to watch. Ivan's face carried a bored expression as he counted the money she'd just handed over. To her, the money would supplement her meagre state pension and having to give it up meant she wouldn't eat tonight; to him, it was just another line entry in Popov's ledger. Andy carefully avoided eye contact and kept his gaze low. He strode on with more purpose to get clear.

"Hey! Lover Boy!" a voice called from behind and he instantly recognised Popov's sarcastic tone. He didn't stop, or turn, he ran … fast! He could hear the loud footsteps of the thugs behind him as he quickly climbed the steps onto the street towards Kazan Cathedral hoping to lose them in the mass of excited picture-taking tourists. He also hoped the enhanced police presence in the area would make them break their pursuit.

As he reached the Cathedral he turned and saw only two of Popov's thugs behind him. The same two who'd chased after him yesterday. In twenty-four hours their fitness hadn't improved as the distance between them had widened. Andy continued past the Cathedral heading into the Gum Shopping Mall.

Once inside the Mall, he took the stairs up to the next level and sprinted along the narrow walkway which overlooked the central atrium. About halfway along, he bolted left into a store and came to a halt, immediately regretting his choice as he faced several female mannequins dressed in various styles and colours of women's underwear; it was lingerie store! *I can't walk out now or I'll attract unnecessary attention*, he thought, as he did his best to look interested in the merchandise. After a few moments an attractive young shop assistant wearing perfectly applied make-up approached him. He smiled at her.

"How may I help you? Do you have something already in mind?" she asked in Russian.

"Yes, it's my girlfriend's birthday next week and I wanted to …" Andy blushed as he paused, he delivered his Russian fluently, but still with an American accent.

"Give her a surprise?" she finished his sentence.

"Yes. I want to surprise her and make her feel special." They both laughed.

"Is she a Russian girl?" the assistant enquired.

"Yes." Andy lied.

"Then she's very lucky you found us, we must make her present very special," the assistant had switched to English.

She wants to impress me. "That's why I'm here," Andy smiled and gestured with his hand in a theatrical wave.

For the next twenty minutes Andy and the assistant discussed the merits of the different female lingerie sets. He gained an entire education on what modern Russian women like from their underwear to their lovers. More than once he nearly forgot his fictional cover story and had to stop himself from asking for her number. He'd had the presence of mind to move deeper into the store and away from the direct line of sight of the glass storefront whilst maintaining a view of the passing foot traffic in the Mall. No Popov or Ivan and his pals.

When he left the store Andy was in possession of a small bag containing a very expensive set of black silk lingerie and he wondered how much of this he could put on a J101F without needing too much explanation.

CHAPTER 8

The senior administrator of the '*Ports and Aerodrome Department*' had nearly finished reading his daily newspaper when a loud knock at his door rudely interrupted him. His staff knew not to disturb him before eleven unless urgent.

"Come!" he commanded.

One of his office juniors opened the door and entered. "Sir, I have someone from the Investigative Branch to see you, it's Colonel Shanina!" the junior informed him.

Yuri Stepanov had been an FSB agent for over twenty years and had spent most of his career posted to the remotest and coldest parts of Russia. He had a suspicion it was because of his father who had been detained for '*undisclosed activities against the interests of the state*' as a result of which he'd spent six years in a Siberian Gulag where each harsh winter he nearly froze to death. Yuri had never been given the opportunity to become an officer but had been grateful for each of his promotions to his current position.

"Show him in," Stepanov instructed. Stepanov stood as Colonel Shanina entered his office. The Colonel had a good five inches on him and was impeccably dressed in a well-tailored suit with matching designer white shirt and red tie. Stepanov wore a crumpled brown suit, white shirt and cheap dark red tie which showed a small yellow stain.

The two men shook hands. "Please, sit," Stepanov directed the Colonel to a chair opposite his cluttered desk.

"Thank you for seeing me without an appointment," the Colonel said.

"You're welcome. How can I help?"

"I can't go into much detail. All you need to know is I'm leading an active investigation. I need to see the FSB duty rosters for the ports of Saint Petersburg, Vladivostok and Murmansk for the last six months. I also want to see who is rostered on for the next month."

"Certainly, we have all of the historical records so I can easily get this for you. I personally approve all rosters so I can tell you who is detailed to be working at each of those locations over the next month."

"Good. I'll wait while you get them."

Stepanov's smile slipped for a moment as he picked up the handset from his yellow desk phone and dialled the number of the office junior. He knew this task would take hours during which he would be left 'entertaining' this senior officer from the IB. After issuing his instructions to the office junior, he put the phone down and smiled at the Colonel.

***

To open the heavy wooden doors required more effort than Andy expected to gain entry to the Moscow Chamber Opera Theatre off Nikolskaya Street. Once inside, Andy found the temperature pleasantly cool. He looked around. With its high vaulted ceilings and bright blue décor Andy thought the theatre highly ornate and, for a historic building in Russia, surprisingly well-maintained.

Andy moved further into the theatre but, although his footsteps clattered loudly on the wooden parquet flooring in the entrance hall, he didn't seem to be attracting any immediate attention. *All good so far*, he thought as he approached the reception area and glanced inside; it was empty. As Andy continued deeper into the theatre, the wooden parquet flooring gave way to bright blue carpet, which perfectly matched the color of the walls and ceiling.

He briefly looked at his reflection in a wall-to-wall mirror before moving into the main auditorium where he stopped in his tracks. The auditorium oozed elegance with its large stage and seating areas which reached up into the galleries way above him. The expansive use of bright blue gave the theatre a feeling of opulence from another era.

Andy gave credit to the Communists for their heavy investment in the arts as a way to provide entertainment for the Party Elite. He thought the performers may have lived less privileged lives and earned peanuts, but they were probably grateful they were not digging coal or uranium from the mines or working on a collective farm in all weathers.

Andy jumped with surprise when he turned to find a middle-aged bearded man, standing not two meters away, staring at him. *Where the hell did he spring from?* he thought as he composed himself. Wearing scruffy jeans and a grubby black tee-shirt, the man smelled strongly of stale tobacco and alcohol.

"What are you doing in here?" the man demanded in Russian.

"I'm organising a tour for a group of American tourists and I've been asked to find a theatre with a suitable performance for them to attend. It's this week." Andy replied in his best poor Russian.

"Why didn't you phone reception instead of coming inside and sneaking around?"

"I did phone, but no-one picked up, so I thought I'd come here and take a look for myself."

"We do have a performance this week: 'The Magic Flute'. I'm in charge of lighting. I don't do tours. Come back when there's someone on reception."

Andy reached into his wallet and produced a twenty-dollar bill. "I'm really short on time. Can you show me around?" With little hesitation the man pocketed the money, introduced himself as Igor and indicated Andy should follow him quickly through a side door.

To Andy's surprise the tour lasted nearly thirty minutes and went better than expected as Igor showed him around all of the backstage areas, including the dressing rooms and the trap doors in the stage. Igor was enjoying himself and, as a bonus, showed Andy how the trap door mechanism worked.

"I think this might be the right place," Andy said as though totally engrossed. "Any issues if I sleep on this overnight and maybe come back tomorrow?" Igor nodded but looked perplexed, he didn't think selecting a theatre performance for a bunch of tourists was such an intensive undertaking. Andy saw the hesitation and produced another twenty-dollar bill. "Thanks you've been a great help," he said handing the note to Igor.

He turned and left the theatre not waiting to see Igor pocket the bill.

CHAPTER 9

Andy took a circuitous route back to the safe house during which he doubled back on himself and continuously checked for tails. By the time he reached the apartment complex he was confident he had no tails following him.

It was three in the afternoon and Tex had sprawled himself across the double sofa, his feet draped over one arm, his shoulders and head over the other. He screamed at the television while watching a football game. The volume set to maximum, making the commentary and stadium noise almost deafening. The game still had a quarter to go and the Patriots were trailing.

"Come on guys … get it to the quarterback … snap it back … Noooo!" Tex screamed at the screen. He looked surprised at Andy's unexpected arrival and immediately put the game on pause; the apartment fell silent until Tex spoke: "You're back early."

"I've got a lot on at the moment." Tex sat up from the sofa and listened as Andy continued, "I have to plan for an op and tonight I'm meeting with an asset."

"Hey buddy, I feel really bad about the stuff-up the other day near the Archives building when I was late. I want to make it up to you. Is there anything I can do to help?"

Andy thought for a moment, "Yeah, you can make dinner while I work."

"Deal." Tex looked at his watch. "What time are you out tonight?"

"I'll be leaving before eight, the meet is at ten."

"Okay buddy. I'll get back to the game with the volume down, while you work, and later I'll make us a spaghetti bolognaise."

"Sounds fine to me." Andy made his way to the dining room table where he spread out his note books, various maps, transport time tables and reference guides. "Did you check the security footage or sweep the place today?" Andy asked just as Tex reached for the remote.

"No," came the response. Andy seethed inwardly as it had been Tex's responsibility this week to review the security footage of the apartment and sweep the place for transmitting devices. Tex hit play, turned the volume down and resumed his interest in the big game without a care in the world.

Andy headed for the security suite. The name was a rather grand title for a room not much larger than a broom closet. Andy stepped inside, closed the door behind him and sat down in the single black swivel chair.

On the wall were five screens: the top left showed the front door from a hidden camera across the corridor; the top right, a view from inside the apartment from an oblique angle showing the door from the inside; the main part of the room and kitchen were on the middle screen; bottom left, the feed from across the street and a good twenty meters either side of the front entrance to the complex; and, the final screen, played feed taken from the roof showing the alley to the rear of the apartment building.

Andy grabbed the keyboard and keyed in the date and time of the last review. The screens went dark for several seconds before showing their respective views. Andy selected 'fast forward' and watched as the images moved at fifty times their normal playing time. His particular focus was the footage from the apartment. He also looked to spot anything unusual from the other screens.

This part of the job he found to be a regular pain in the butt, but it needed to be done; he didn't want to work on his extraction plan only for the Russians to be closely monitoring everything. Over the last three hours nothing had caught his attention and no one other than Tex and him had been in the apartment. Andy emerged from the security suite and rubbed his eyes with his left hand. In his right hand he carried a state-of-the art spectrum analyser. He switched on the analyser in search of electronic transmissions from their vicinity.

Tex had moved from the sofa and was busy in the kitchen. The smells indicated he had the food preparation well underway. "I'm doing some garlic bread. That okay with you?"

"Sure."

"Anything on the tapes?"

"All clear."

"Great! Chow will be ready in fifteen."

Andy looked at the display on the spectrum analyser. Tex was using the microwave and Andy could see a clear signal spike from it. "Hey, just turn that off a second," Andy asked. Tex paused the microwave and the signal spike at two-point-four-five gigahertz disappeared. "All good, you can switch it back on."

Tex hit 'Start' and the microwave whirred back to life; the signal spike returned. Andy powered down the spectrum analyser and returned it to its shelf in the security suite. Andy calmly sat at the table in front of his paperwork, but under the surface he fumed, *I've just spent three hours doing your job and you didn't even budge when you knew the sweep needed to be done. You're an asshole!* Andy decided he'd put in for a change of accommodation, without Tex, once he'd completed his current assignment.

"Hey buddy. You don't want to be doing that. You need to clear that away and set the table. Chow is almost ready...' that was it, Tex had just pressed all the right buttons. Andy stood up, walked across the space between them and looked up directly into Tex's eyes allowing his frustration to boil over.

"Tex, I wanted to work this afternoon, instead, I've been looking at three hours of security footage and doing the weekly electronic sweep. Those were your only jobs to do today!"

Tex looked hurt. "Hey buddy, I forgot," he held out both his arms, palms upwards as if asking for divine forgiveness, "if I thought it my turn. I would have done it." Tex rubbed his nose as he dropped his arms.

"I'm so far behind, it's not funny."

"I'm sorry buddy." he sounded genuine, he always did. "What can I do to help? Come on, let me make it up to you."

"You could help by driving me tonight. I'm meeting The Colonel at Gorky Park on the north side of Leninsky Avenue. You can drop me off on Krymsky by the bridge a couple of blocks away, so I can check for any tails, and you can pick me up afterwards across the road at the carpark at Gorky Park Towers. That would give me back a few hours."

"Done."

"We'll leave at nine."

CHAPTER 10

Tex didn't look comfortable as he squeezed into Andy's yellow Lada, his head scraped against the interior of the car's roof and, even with the seat right back, his bent knees brushed against the bottom of the steering wheel. Tex found driving quite a challenge in such a small car as they made their way across Moscow.

At twenty–past nine Tex briefly stopped the car on Krymsky just across the bridge over the Moscow River. Andy jumped out and spoke to Tex as he closed the door: "Remember, pick me up from Gorky Park Tower carpark at ten–twenty. Drive in and, if I'm not there, drive out, circle round and come back at ten–thirty. If I'm still not there, come back at ten–forty–five, after that head back to the safe house and I'll make my own way back."

"Got it buddy."

Andy watched as Tex pulled away and the car's lights disappeared into the distance. With Tex gone, Andy headed down the stone steps which led from the road to the river bank. He followed the walkway under the bridge towards one of the park's northern entrances. The night air had an unexpected chill to it and, being this close to the river, felt damp. Andy shivered and made sure the zip on his lightweight jacket was fully done up before driving his hands deep into his pockets.

He walked briskly in the darkness making his way from lamppost to lamppost using the small islands of light they cast on the ground to guide him along the path. Andy found the park wasn't as deserted as he'd hoped it would be as he passed two dog walkers, a few people taking a shortcut through the park and a courting couple who sought privacy for their intimate encounter. Fifteen minutes later, standing to the side of a tall pine tree, Andy had a position overlooking the south entrance, off Titovsky. His eyes had gained their night vision and the area looked quiet.

The distant chime from a church bell told him it was ten o'clock. Moments later a tall figure, being led by a large dog pulling on its lead, came into the park. Andy felt certain it was his man. To double check, he concentrated on the sounds of the night. He listened to the dog's rapid panting as it strained on the leash, next were the footsteps of the dog walker, and, finally, road noise carried in from outside the park. He looked around once more to confirm visually they were alone and, as the figure approached, he stepped from the shadows and waited on the path. The dog snarled and closed in on Andy as it strained on its lead.

"Kazak. No!" The dog was pulled back as its lead was snatched back.

Recognizing The Colonel's voice Andy spoke, "Do you walk Kazak every night?"

"Most nights, it gives me a routine and makes me difficult to follow," he paused, " ... also, it helps my neighbor out."

"I'm working on a plan to create a diversion for when you make your move."

"I need this to be soon, Malchik is getting closer."

"How soon can you move?" Andy asked.

"Two days."

"Okay, remember that you're responsible for getting out of the country and making your way to Amsterdam."

Before The Colonel could respond, Andy picked up the sounds of rapidly moving footsteps from the direction The Colonel had entered the park. There were at least two people, running in heavy footwear, not sneakers, Andy instinctively backed into the shadows of the tree. "Go!" Andy hissed.

The Colonel calmly walked away with an enthusiastic Kazak trying to drag him forward faster than The Colonel intended. Andy watched as two figures passed his position and quickly closed in on The Colonel. *I hope they don't have flash lights*, he thought, as he knew he would be easy to spot behind the tree. The Colonel was a good fifty meters away by the time the men caught up with him. Andy could hear their voices as they carried easily in the cold night air.

"Colonel Shanina?"

"Yes?"

"Moscow Militia. We have received reports of increased criminal activity in the park at night," said one.

"Robberies, assaults, that kind of thing ...," cut in the second.

"We heard you were coming to the park and we wanted to make sure you were safe," the first voice stated as sincerely as he could muster. Andy wasn't fooled by the 'co-incidence' nor did he think The Colonel would be as easily fooled either.

Andy heard a vehicle pull up from the direction The Colonel and two men had entered the park. He shifted his position slightly and saw, from the light emitted by nearby streetlights, four men step from the vehicle and enter the park. Andy could see the figures moving to form an extended line; the conversation with The Colonel continued behind him.

"We'll escort you through the park. Think of us as your ... personal security detail."

"Most kind of you, but as you see I have a large dog." Andy heard The Colonel's voice and was impressed with how calm and even it sounded. *Years of practice in this country where your friend could just as easily turn out to be your enemy for the right price*, he thought. Andy heard the sound of forced laughter.

"Your dog won't stop a nine-millimetre round at close range as the mugger demands your wallet!"

Andy knew The Colonel had no choice but to allow the men to accompany him on his walk. As he watched The Colonel move further away, Andy caught a glimpse of further movement in front of the trio. It looked like there were at least a half-dozen figures moving ahead of The Colonel; the figures had fanned out with blinding flash lights sweeping from side to side towards Andy and the four men behind him. He closed his left eye to preserve at least some of his night vision.

Shit! he said to himself as he realised the four men were acting as 'beaters' driving their quarry, him, towards the trap which they set with the line of men in front. Andy didn't have time to dwell on his situation, he had two options: get clear or risk being captured.

He bent double and kept low, using the darkness and well-developed trees and shrubs lining the path to conceal his movement, as he ran away from the danger. He knew he had to avoid the footpaths as they were darker in contrast to the grass and surrounding shrubs making it easier to spot movement ... and the sound of his footsteps would be amplified. He hoped the guys with the flash lights would be dependent on seeing only within the wide beams of their torch lights. If he could stay out of their sweeping beams, he'd be relatively safe from detection, but Andy had to stay on this side of the park and not be pushed in the other direction towards the waiting reception party.

Crouched and moving slowly, it took Andy several tense minutes to outflank the 'beaters'. He knew there was no point in leaving via one of the park entrances as all the entrances were most likely being watched. With the beams behind him, he headed for the park fence which stood at nearly nine feet. He picked a spot along the perimeter where there was a tall tree with thick branches some of which were overhanging the fence. The tree's dense foliage offered another bonus as it blotted out the nearest street lights from Leninsky Avenue, making anyone near the tree, practically invisible.

Andy reached the wide tree trunk and jumped to reach the lowest branch. He pulled himself up and for additional leverage, used his legs to kick against the bow of the tree. Once perched on the lower branch, Andy climbed up to the next set of thick branches. He stopped, looked around and listened. He could easily make out the line of flashlights sweeping and moving further away. The traffic, now a few metres away, generated the only noise he could hear and would mask the sound of his landing. Andy steadied his breathing as he felt his heart pounding in his chest.

All looks clear, he told himself as he edged along one of the larger branches which overhung the fence. Above the sidewalk on the outside of the park, Andy gripped the branch, swung his legs down and extended his arms moving him closer to the ground before he released his grip. The Physical Training Instructors at The Farm had trained them to bend their knees when falling from a height and roll with the impact; he executed the move smoothly and with one fluid movement was back on his feet and walking away. To anyone not paying close attention Andy had just appeared out of thin air.

Andy crossed the road to be on the same side as the Gorky Park Tower. He checked his watch, it was approaching ten–thirty. Tex would be making his approach for the second pick-up attempt. *So far, so good.* As Andy neared the pick-up point, he saw the familiar color and shape of his Lada as it arrived and entered the carpark in front of the Tower. Relieved that Tex had been true to his word, Andy started to move towards the relative safety of the car but with less than one block to cover, all hell broke loose.

Cars appeared, to the front and rear, immediately boxing in the Lada; Tex was stuck with nowhere to go. Figures jumped from other cars, swarming towards the Lada … and Tex. *Get out!* Andy screamed in his head. Two militia cars with flashing red lights screeched to a halt disgorging their uniformed passengers who proceeded to also surround the car. Andy had drifted back into the shadows but was still close enough to see the look of surprised panic on Tex's face. There was nothing Andy could do but watch the unfolding scene.

"This is the Security Services. Place your hands where we can see them on the steering wheel," a voice commanded. Andy knew Tex struggled with the tiny space in the car and saw him drop his hands out of view and looked, to Andy at least, like he was trying to push the seat backwards before moving to raise his hands.

"Pistolet!" a voice shouted from the crowd.

Almost as one, the figures surrounding the car opened fire. As the glass shattered and the doors popped with holes, Tex's body jolted and jerked as if it was being struck rapidly by a high voltage cattle prod. His head exploded, his jawbone vanished, as round after round tore into him. Andy continued to watch, helplessly glued to the horrific scene, as Tex was brutally murdered. Then he saw a spark flash inside the Lada and, seconds later, flames quickly spread across the bullet torn interior engulfing Tex and the car completely; if Tex wasn't dead he soon would be and burnt to a crisp.

"Fire! Fire!" he heard a voice call out.

The shooting stopped. The rapport from the last shots echoed off the buildings, leaving an eerie silence to settle on the scene.

"Let the Yankee burn!" came the reply.

What? the voice had the effect of snapping Andy out of his daze and returning him to real time. He should have left the scene immediately, but his anger and curiosity got the better of him; he wanted to find out who had uttered those words. It was easier than expected to pick out the speaker as a figure stepped forward to take a closer look at the burning vehicle. Satisfied that the 'person' inside was still there, and wasn't going to walk away, the figure turned to address the shooters.

"Call the Fire Brigade and move back from here. The fuel tank is likely to blow."

"Yes, sir!" one of the men replied.

The light from the burning car illuminated the figure. He was young, with short, dark hair and well dressed.

"Lieutenant Malchik. What do you want us to do about Colonel Shanina?"

"Let him go about his business. We can play with him for a few more days before we arrest him for his crimes against the State. With Flint dead, his plans will have been derailed. He isn't going anywhere soon."

CHAPTER 11

Andy watched the approaching fire trucks stop and set about the task of putting out the car fire. He heard the wailing sirens as more militia vehicles arrived at the scene. He'd seen enough, there was nothing he could do for Tex; he needed to get clear to avoid being swept up in any follow-up operation for witnesses or, worse, being identified by Malchik.

Andy turned and walked away from the blazing vehicle; its dancing flames still bright enough to cast shadows in front of him. He looked back over his shoulder, despite the efforts of the firemen, thick black smoke bellowed from the fire and climbed with burning orange embers high into the night sky.

He moved away from Leninsky Avenue taking turns, right, left and right, not thinking about his direction, hoping he was putting enough space between him and any potential tail. *How did Malchik know about the meeting? Malchik thought I had been in the car. Malchik wanted me dead.* Andy's thoughts were jumbled and unclear.

He wanted to lose himself in the city, never to be found. In the darkness he recognised the Donskoy Monastery and stopped to look at the looming structure. The mind works in strange ways when under extreme stress, and for Andy, the history of the building came into his mind: established in 1591 it became the site of an uprising during the plague riots in 1771; ransacked by Napoleon's army in 1812 it was closed after the October Revolution in 1917; used as a penal colony for children in 1924 before returning to its current cloistered monastic use. A turbulent past, but now, as he stood there in silence he felt the peace and tranquillity radiate out towards him; he slowed his breathing and calmed himself allowing the darkness to keep him safe for the moment.

Andy gained control of his expanding thoughts and locked them back in their box, before he continued his journey back to the safe house. The initial shock had subsided leaving Andy focussed and alert. He knew he only had a few hours before the fatigue would kick in and needed to use this narrow window to ensure his own safety.

Andy took the pedestrian walkway on the Novoandreevsky Bridge to cross back over the Moscow River; the bridge's thick steel girders and solid structure offered a feeling of security and relative safety from the speeding cars on the adjacent highway. After crossing onto the far bank of the river, Andy hailed a passing cab, the driver pulled over grateful for the fare, and more so, when Andy gave his destination across the other side of the city.

The driver, Alexi was talkative and told Andy he came from Georgia and had lived in Moscow for eight years. By the end of the journey Andy knew about the Alexi's life story and of his family left back home in Georgia. With two relatively well paying 'cash-in-hand' jobs he sent money at the end of each month to support his wife, kids and her parents. He had a young girlfriend in Moscow who was three months pregnant which meant he had no plans to return home anytime soon. Andy gave Alexi a healthy tip as the driver dropped him a block away from the safe house.

Without further excitement he reached the safe house and relaxed slightly once he'd triple locked the door behind him. He picked up the secure line and called the Duty Officer at the Embassy. At this hour it would be quiet and the Duty Officer was probably reading a book or catching up on paperwork. Either way Andy didn't believe they'd be rushed off their feet.

While Andy waited for the Duty Officer to answer, he looked around the apartment. He felt a lump form in his throat as he saw constant reminders of Tex; from remnants of their last supper together through to his clothing which he'd discarded in the living room. Tex had promised to pick it up and launder it when they got back that night. *Some promises are just not kept.*

Andy could see into Tex's bedroom, then averted his gaze as the call connected. "Duty Officer, Shapiro, how can I assist?" a rather bored sounding voice answered the phone.

"This is Andrew Flint from the Overseas Aid Analytics Department. I need to report a major incident."

"Please confirm your ID number?" any trace of 'boredom' had quickly evaporated.

"Five, three, two, eight, two, two, black," Andy replied immediately.

"Check digits, one eight," came the authentication challenge.

"Check digits, zero two," Andy replied

"You are authenticated," the Duty Officer stated, "I can confirm your line is secure, please tell me about the major incident and let's get you some help."

"At ten this evening I had a scheduled meeting with an asset at Gorky Park when we were compromised by the Russian Security Services. I evaded detection, however, the Russians stopped Agent Tex Striker at the pick-up point in the adjacent carpark, and shot him dead."

"Confirm, 'Agent Tex Striker is dead'," Shapiro asked.

"Yes. I confirm." Andy replied.

"Please, continue."

Andy could hear Shapiro typing furiously. He knew the call was being recorded at the Embassy; a copy would be automatically encrypted and sent in real time to Langley. He repeated his statement, this time a bit slower so that Shapiro could keep up: "The Russian Security Services blocked the car Tex was driving so he couldn't extract himself from the situation. He was told to raise his hands and as he attempted to do so it was misinterpreted and someone shouted he had a gun. Then, with the car surrounded, they opened fired and shot him multiple times."

"Can you confirm Agent Striker is dead?" Shapiro repeated.

Andy's patience evaporated as he lost his cool "Yes. About ten guys with guns shot him from about 5 meters away. They emptied their magazines and reloaded. The car burst into flames and Tex didn't get out from the inferno."

"Could he have survived?" Shapiro asked.

Jeez are you really that stupid or do I need to come over and type the damn report myself, Andy thought as he attempted to calm himself down: "If Tex is bullet proof, doesn't need a head or an intact brain to function, and is fireproof at up to two thousand degrees, then yes, he could have survived."

Shapiro fell silent for a moment as though he was thinking how to calm Andy down but instead he just asked another inane question: "Are you being sarcastic?"

"No. I don't think so. Do you?" Andy spat back barely controlling his anger at the constant stream of daft questions from this inept desk jockey.

Shapiro paused before continuing, "OK Andrew, let's not get personal, I have a job to do. I'm here to help. We need to understand whether this is an extraction or recovery operation. Where did you say the shooting took place?"

Andy breathed deeply and calmed down before he spoke: "The carpark at Gorky Park Tower, off Leninsky Avenue. The car's registered to me. The Russian FSB believe I'm the person who died at the scene."

"OK Andrew, I have Carrie Roper on the line, she's going to join the call."

"Hi Andrew, what the bloody hell happened?" Carrie asked, her voice unusually slow and somewhat deeper, as though she'd just been disturbed from a deep, comfortable sleep. Andy went through the incident again; Carrie and Shapiro listened without any interruptions.

As he finished he said, "We have a serious opponent. An FSB officer called Oleg Malchik. He knew about the meeting and expected me to be there. He believes I'm dead, not Tex."

Carrie spoke next, "Thanks Andrew, I'm going to speak with Langley and we'll get back to you once we have a plan to sort this mess out." The line went dead. Andy replaced the receiver and sat quietly for a few minutes, his head buried in his hands, as he replayed Tex's last terrifying moments. The sound of the phone ringing brought him back to the present.

"Hello?"

"Andrew Flint, this is Greg Harrison in Langley. I've been briefed on what happened and I need to hear it from you." Andy realised this was the Greg with whom Carrie had been speaking earlier that day which now felt like a lifetime ago. Andy knew this wasn't going to be an easy conversation. "Start from the beginning." Andy repeated the evening's events in as much detail as possible for Greg and at the end Greg said, "Thank you Andrew. It can't have been easy to see your colleague gunned down in front of you."

"No, Sir, it wasn't."

"There is one thing which bothers me," Greg said, Andy sat up alert – he'd heard the change in Greg's tone – he knew he had to listen careful as Greg continued, "didn't you get the message this meet wasn't to go ahead? I thought I'd been crystal clear with Carrie. Didn't she pass that instruction on?"

"No, Sir, my instructions were to meet with the asset and provide information so he could gain our protection once outside of Eastern Europe."

"Well there's going to be an investigation to find out why the communication didn't get through to you particularly as it resulted in the death of a field agent. You're new in the field aren't you?"

"Yes, I am."

"Pity, we're short of good field agents."

The line went dead.

CHAPTER 12

The sound of a ringing phone disturbed Andy from his deep sleep; he checked his watch, just after six in the morning, he'd had three hours sleep. Andy yawned, stretched and made his way to the secure phone and picked it up.

"Jack Masters, FBI. Is that Andrew Flint?"

"Yes." Andy was confused. *The FBI. Must be on the case to investigate the murder of a Federal employee, while on duty.*

"Are you alone?" Masters asked.

"Yes, I am."

"Okay. You're going to need to sit down as this call isn't going to be easy. I'm with the Counter-Espionage Investigative Branch."

"What's this got to do with Tex's murder?" Andy asked as he was already confused.

"I'll come to that in a minute. What I want to discuss with you is a matter of national security and is not to be discussed with anyone apart from me. Is that clear?"

"How do I know you're legit?" Andy asked.

"Are you trying to obstruct justice?" Masters snapped back.

"As far as I know you're a voice I've never heard of before on the end of a secure phone."

The line went quiet as Masters worked out what to do next. "Okay, if it helps, call the FBI main number and ask for the Director of Counter-Espionage."

Andy hung up and dialled Langley's main number and asked the operator to assist by putting his call through to the FBI. "Connecting you now, Sir," the CIA operator announced as the destination started to ring. "Federal Bureau of Investigation, how may I direct your call?" the next operator asked.

"Director of Counter-Espionage, please."

"One moment, Sir," the line went quiet, before it started to ring.

"Jack Masters, Director of Counter-Espionage."

"Okay, I believe you are who you claim to be."

"Then let me start by saying I'm sorry about Tex, I heard you two were good buddies, so I can imagine you're going through a rough patch." – *Not quite buddies, I was planning to move out,* Andy thought – Masters continued, "we believe there is at least one mole at the Agency working for the Russians."

"Are you sure?"

"We've been investigating this for over a year and The Colonel knows who they are."

"Why all of the rush right now?"

"The FSB officer you came across last night, Malchik, has recently gained access to the mole and used them to close down our eyes and ears in Russia. You know we regularly share intelligence with our allies and our allies share theirs with us, right?"

"Yes, Sir," Andy confirmed.

"That's how our allies were compromised. Someone at the Agency is helping the Russians. The Colonel believes he's been betrayed and that Malchik is closing in on him."

"He told me about Malchik at our first meeting. What do you expect from me? I'm the new guy, remember?" Andy said with a bit of edge to his tone. He had a good idea where the conversation was going, but he needed Masters to say it out loud … *just for the record,* Andy told himself.

"The FBI wants The Colonel in the United States as soon as possible. This means you're going against your chain of command. That's why you can't discuss this matter with anyone at the Agency."

Andy sat in silence. Extreme fatigue meant his thinking was slow as he considered his predicament. "Since I can't speak to anyone at The Agency, is there anyone in Moscow I can call on for assistance?" Andy asked.

There was a long paused from Masters. "Yes, the US Ambassador in Moscow, he's a good friend of the FBI, I'll brief him that you are part of a parallel operation."

"Thanks."

"What's the plan with The Colonel?" Masters asked.

"In two days he'll make his way to our Embassy in Amsterdam where he'll surrender into our custody."

"Does the CIA know the plan?"

"No. I haven't shared the plan with anyone yet," Andy replied, in truth he was still working on the details.

"Good, don't tell them anything. I'll arrange for my agents to be at the Embassy in Amsterdam to receive The Colonel when he presents himself."

"Okay."

"Andrew, good luck!"

"Thanks!" he said as the line went dead, he'd need every bit of luck going if his plan was to work. With the call over Andy headed back to bed for extra sleep.

Less than two hours later Andy had showered, dried and dressed. He picked up the phone to call Roper at the Embassy. She answered on the third ring.

"Hi Carrie, it's Andy Flint," he announced.

"Hi Andrew. How are you holding up?" Roper asked.

That's odd she actually sounds concerned. Andy had already thought about his language and speech patterns before the call with Roper. He'd slow it down, add pauses, hesitation and some repetition for effect: "There's been a lot to get my head around from last night … seeing Tex die like that … I need time, yeah time, to think and come to terms with it ... I mean, um, seeing Tex die like that ... I've got to accept he's gone."

"You're right, I'm worried about you," she replied, "you're a victim too." This wasn't what he was expecting at all, he believed she was trying to give the impression that she actually cared about his well-being. Roper continued, "I'll arrange counselling for you to make sure you're coping and you've come to terms with what you witnessed."

"Thanks Carrie ... err, I appreciate your help and concern," Andy felt a lump form in his throat as he briefly thought about Tex and then Roper's supportive response. After a short pause, Andy continued, "since the Russians believe it's me who died last night, why don't we keep it that way for a little while longer? Why make their lives easier, we don't owe them anything do we?"

The line went quiet for a second: "You're right. We don't owe the murdering bastards anything. We'll keep them in the dark as long as possible. They'll know you're alive soon enough when you leave."

"Leave?" he tried not to sound surprised but failed miserably!

"You can't go back into the field until you've completed the psych evaluation and interview with the internal review team investigating the events leading to Tex's death. So you're heading back to Langley and are deskbound for now."

"I see?" Andy realised as soon as he uttered the words, his tone was wrong, it came across as questioning. He jumped in quickly to smooth her over: "All help is welcome. I need to be fit, healthy and focussed one hundred percent on the job and if this gets me there sooner, it can only be a good thing." *Hopefully that sounded more upbeat and agreeable*, he thought, *enough to put her off the scent at least*!

"Andrew, that's the right attitude, many in the Agency, particularly the old guard, would struggle with what you've been through. They'd bottle up their problems, bury them deep in the back of their minds and years later either turn to drink or blow their brains out."

"I understand, but before I'm on the plane, can I take a couple of days to sort through Tex's effects and get them shipped back to his folks."

"Andrew that's kind of you to offer, take the time you need, but be discrete. We don't want the Russian Authorities to find out you're still alive until you're on a flight back to DC, understood?"

"Yes, and thanks Carrie, I've got his folks' address and I'll use the Embassy to return his personal effects back to them," Andy smiled at the ease of buying the time he needed. With the call over Andy headed for the door. He knew he had a busy day ahead and with no car, he'd either have to walk or use the public transport network.

Chapter 13

Andy made good time as he arrived at the theatre. He stepped inside and the cool air that greeted him felt refreshing and welcoming. He walked confidently towards the side door leading back stage and, just as he reached for the handle, a female voice behind him demanded, "Where are you going?"

Andy stopped and spun around to see a young woman staring at him. She looked to be in her early twenties wearing skin-tight black trousers and a black cotton top. Her brown hair was tied immaculately back in a ponytail; he could see that it was long as it fell below her shoulders. She was carrying a box which appeared to contain programmes for the production.

"I'm meeting with Igor. He's expecting me," Andy smiled, his fluent Russian had only a trace of an American accent.

"Okay. Let me put these in the ticket booth and then I'll take you to him. Do you work in theatre?" she asked as she walked to the booth and placed the box of programmes next to the cash register.

"No. Just catching up with my friend."

"You live in Moscow?"

Is she interested in me? Andy thought as he followed her backstage. "I do, but I'm leaving for a few weeks and I'm not sure when I'll be back."

She looked disappointed: "Do you have a girlfriend?"

Wow! She's keen. "No, I'm single," he replied. Andy was pleased the theatre's poor lighting hid the red flush spread across his cheeks.

"Oh, maybe we could meet up if you come back to Moscow?" she suggested

"Er … yes … that would be great," he stammered, "by the way, my name is Andy."

She smiled, "I am called Lenya it is nice to meet you." Their conversation ended when they arrived at Igor's small, untidy workshop filled with an assortment of wires, cables and lights of various types. To one side were stacked different lighting rigs which Andy thought had been used at one time or another in a performance.

"Igor, I have Andy for you," she called out.

"Thanks," Andy replied.

"Look me up when you're back in Moscow."

Andy smiled, "I will."

Lenya turned and left the two men alone.

"I think she likes you," Igor said with a grin.

"Maybe," Andy blushed with embarrassment.

"Will you be bringing your tour here?" Igor asked.

"Yes, I came to get the tickets for tomorrow evening and, in addition, I've been given five hundred dollars if you can help me with something a little bit special for my clients."

Igor slowly rubbed his beard as he thought about the offer. After seeing the way Igor had quickly pocketed the forty dollars the previous day, Andy knew it would be too tempting to turn down more easy money. He wasn't disappointed!

"Let's talk," came the response.

***

Andy sat on a wooden bench watching the crowds of 'out of towners' and tourists taking photos of The Kremlin, Lenin's Tomb and Saint Basil's Basilica. He would never get bored of Red Square. He enjoyed watching people trying to guess, or make up, their life stories. It was a game he'd played as a child when his parents left him for hours alone in the car outside the Roosevelt Mall in Philadelphia.

He admired the different architecture surrounding Red Square marking various periods in the history of the city; the opulence and extravagance of the Tsars as well as the drab and oppressive architecture of the Stalin's era. He couldn't quite believe his good fortune at being posted to Russia and having the opportunity to take in the sights he'd read about at school.

Andy's thoughts drifted to Tex; how sudden and unexpectedly his luck had changed. If Andy hadn't got Tex to drive, he wouldn't have been in Andy's car and he'd still be alive, but he, Andy, would have been toast! After half-an-hour of people watching and reflection, Andy headed back to the Embassy and his appointment with the Ambassador.

When Andy reached the fourth floor he stepped out of the lift and was greeted by the formally quiet atmosphere of the Ambassador's suite. The Ambassador's assistant kept Andy waiting for ten minutes before ushering him into the Ambassador's spacious office.

Ambassador Rushbrooke approached Andy and held out his hand for Andy to shake, which he did, firmly. Before coming to Moscow, Andy had read a report about the Ambassador. A long-time friend of the President – and rumoured to have contributed generously to his successful campaign – he'd been appointed to this high profile and much sought after position as a reward for his support during the lead up to the election.

The report stated the Ambassador had made his enormous fortune in construction with an enviable high-end property portfolio across North America and Europe. It speculated that he was looking to capitalise on the political changes in Russia viewing it as a lucrative growth market for his business. As the US Ambassador, he would certainly gain the influential contacts he'd need to make this a reality.

The Ambassador smiled and gestured for Andy to sit on one of two leather chairs which faced his desk. It was no surprise to Andy that Rushbrooke chose to sit in the larger, higher chair. "Jack Masters called me early this morning and said I should meet with you. Must be important?" the Ambassador said, his pronunciation betraying a slight southern drawl.

"I think so. I'm involved in an operation and last night the FSB, and the Russian police, murdered my colleague in front of me."

"I heard about that. What do they think the Russians were doing? Why would they shoot dead an American?"

"They knew they were shooting an American, I heard them cursing him as he died."

"You were there?" the Ambassador sounded genuinely surprised.

"Yes," Andy broke away from the Ambassador's gaze and looked down at his shoes.

"If it's any consolation, I've made formal protests to both their Ministry of Interior and to their Deputy Prime Minister. I want to hear what they've got to say," the Ambassador sounded pleased with his efforts; Andy knew it would lead nowhere. He looked up and once again locked eyes with the Ambassador.

"I need your help."

The Ambassador looked interested.

***

With his meeting over, Andy headed down to his office on the second floor to clear Tex's desk. The sombre mood hit Andy as he walked across the floor. He noticed a number of the office staff were carrying tissues and wiping their eyes. A few offered their condolences to Andy, others hugged him and wept. He picked up a cardboard box from the stationary cupboard.

Andy started removing Tex's personal effects from his desk starting with two framed photos of Tex: in one, his arms were wrapped around his younger sister, they were smiling, their eyes sparkled with happiness; the second was a head shot of Tex wearing his soccer helmet capturing a moment of focus and determination mid-game with his eyes fixed on his opponent. Next Andy removed his graduation certificate from The Farm. He picked up Tex's coffee cup with the inscription 'No1 brother' and placed it carefully in the box.

Andy scanned the desk and, aside from stationary, there was nothing else to pack so he turned his attention to the desk drawers. There was a well-thumbed guidebook for Moscow and three sporting magazines from home. One thing he didn't expect to find in Tex's desk drawer, a bible. He'd never known Tex to share his beliefs with anyone and didn't even know if Tex attended church; it was the final item he placed in the box.

Andy looked up and momentarily froze on the spot. His senses quickly returned and he ducked behind a partition and dropping out of sight under a desk. Seconds later, Malchik, guided by his host Carrie Roper, walked calmly past Andy's hiding place and into her office.

What the …?

he Colonel stood in his usual spot on the Metro train looking out of the window. He didn't see Andy pproach and stand behind him. Andy issued the start of the authentication code. The Colonel's eply told Andy he wasn't being followed. The Colonel turned to face Andy and looked as if he'd seen a ghost.

What happened at the Park?" Andy demanded, "they murdered a good friend of mine."

Malchik set a trap. He suspected you would attempt to contact me in the park. I underestimated im. I'm sorry."

How did Malchik know it would be me in the park?"

We know who works at your Embassy. We know Manchester is out of the country. Roper isn't a ield agent and you were the new pain in the ass. Malchik figured you'd be the Agency contact. His nen identified you from the other day on the Metro. That gave him the confirmation he needed."

Why kill Tex?"

He thought," The Colonel hesitated, "no, he still thinks, that it was you in the car. The execution vas payback for the file you stole. In addition, he thinks that he's disrupted the plans for my efection." The Colonel talked calmly, as though Tex's murder didn't matter. Andy felt a rage urning within; he knew he needed to control his anger.

Why should I help you?" Andy asked, "are you really worth it?"

he Colonel looked surprised at being challenged and casually checked no one was within earshot: "I eep a great many secrets. I know of three reliable sources we have in your own Agency. I can tell ou the name of a Senator who is being blackmailed by his Russian mistress to make your iovernment more sympathetic towards Russia and our interests," The Colonel leaned closer and ontinued, "We have people at Boeing, Lockheed Martin and IBM as well as two high level assets vithin the British SIS ... who share every secret you provide them so we can manipulate situations to ur advantage. I can tell you who they are once I am safely out of the country." The Colonel stood up traight and moved away to give Andy some space and allow his words to sink in before finishing vith, "Don't let your colleague's murder have been for nothing, by assisting me you will enable the BI to arrest the traitors and, maybe, turn them into double agents"

ndy clung tightly to the leather grip strap as the train swayed and jolted while he processed his ptions. It all sounded too black and white in a world where there were many shades of grey. He espised The Colonel who was willing to sell his soul to highest bidder to save his own skin, there vas no honour involved, it was just business. But Andy was a pragmatist, if he'd joined the CIA to neet people who were all squeaky clean and honourable, he was in the wrong job. With his decision nade, he turned to face The Colonel: "Okay. It's on. Can you get out of the country tomorrow ight?"

I have a plan," came the reply.

As part of the decoy, book last minute tickets on the midnight Lufthansa flight to Frankfurt."

Okay. Anything else?"

"Yes. Tomorrow night wear your usual overcoat and hat."

"Very well."

"Oh, and one more thing, and this is important, go to the bench nearest to St Basil's Basilica on Red Square. Underneath, on the right side, are instructions on how we'll lose Malchik."

The train entered the next station and came to a stop; the doors opened and The Colonel stepped onto the platform quickly becoming invisible among the throng of evening commuters.

t hadn't turned nine in the evening when the Colonel entered the now quiet offices of the 'Ports and Aerodrome' Department. The Colonel gave a firm knock on Yuri Stepanov's closed office door. After a long pause he heard Stepanov shout, "Come!" Unaware of what was going to greet him on the other side of the door the Colonel took a deep breath, opened the door and entered.

A newspaper lay to the left side of Stepanov's desk, a half-drunk coffee sat resting on a coaster to the right of his desk and in the middle were files set to give the impression he'd been working through them. Stepanov wasn't expecting the Colonel and couldn't hide his look of surprise.

"Yuri. I'm sorry to disturb you, but I thought it important to see you in person."

Stepanov's surprised expression changed to one of confusion: "What important matter do you have to discuss?" Stepanov gestured for the Colonel to sit.

"The files you gave me access to have been very useful. They helped us make significant progress on our investigation and I'm pleased to say we'll be making arrests soon."

Stepanov smiled. "Can I ask what it's in relation to?" he asked.

"I'm afraid not." Stepanov looked disappointed. The Colonel was unmoved and ignoring the look continued, "I can tell you we will be making arrests in Moscow tomorrow morning and in Saint Petersburg the following day." Stepanov leaned forward, clearly interested in what the Colonel had to say. "To make the operation run smoothly, I need you to send a message to your team leader in Saint Petersburg, I believe it is Boris Nevich tomorrow night?"

Stepanov hung off each word: "Yes, it is Nevich. You aren't arresting him, are you? He's one of the few hardworking ones up there!" Stepanov looked worried.

"No, it's not Nevich," The Colonel reassured him.

Stepanov sat back relieved: "What message would you like me to send to Nevich?"

"Tell him to expect my visit in the next two days. Instruct him to give me access to all areas and to give me his full cooperation."

"Okay," Stepanov smiled clearly relieved Nevich wasn't the target of The Colonel's operation.

The Colonel rummaged in the black holdall he'd been carrying when he entered the office. "Ah, here it is!" The Colonel removed six large bottles of vodka and placed them on Stepanov's desk. The Colonel watched Stepanov's face light up with delight and continued, "this is for you to share with your team, tomorrow night, to celebrate the success of our operation. Your part in it has been critical."

Stepanov sat up with his chest puffed out: "Thank you, Colonel, it's more than I'd have ever expected. It will give me great pleasure to share it with my team."

"Tomorrow, I want you to make a toast about your help in cracking our important case."

"I will, now, I'll send your message."

The Colonel stood and left Stepanov's office.

43

The Colonel stepped out of the building onto the sidewalk heading towards Red Square. He doubled back on himself twice checking for tails before dumping the empty holdall in a garbage bin where he knew there were no cameras watching the street.

Even with the detours, Colonel Shanina reached Red Square in twenty minutes. The Colonel turned up his collar as a cold wind swirled around the large open space; today had been much cooler and windier than previous days which meant fewer sightseers. Confident he wasn't being followed he headed for the wooden bench at the far end of the square as instructed by the young American and with a casual glance checked there were no *'watchers'* lurking nearby.

The Colonel was relieved to find the bench unoccupied save for a big fat pigeon pecking at the remains of a burger bun someone had carelessly discarded. He sat and tried to look relaxed as he spread out the newspaper he'd bought from a street kiosk earlier that day. Although it was late the lampposts surrounding the Square were lit so brightly it easy to read the main articles: The forthcoming referendum recommending the people should vote for prosperity and security by backing the motion; Two columns dedicated to Yeltsin and a speech he delivered on his vision to reform the country; Finally, a small article on Saddam Hussain crushing an uprising in Basra by killing the terrorists and criminals who'd led it.

While appearing to be engrossed in the newspaper, the Colonel constantly scanned the area to confirm he wasn't being watched. Satisfied there were no eyes on him, he positioned the open newspaper to create a screen to hide his hand as he felt under the seat. *There it is*, he thought as his fingers touched the envelope. He briefly looked around the square again then tugged hard to free the envelope. He studied the outside for a brief moment before deftly opening it with one hand while still holding on to the newspaper as a screen with the other. Inside was a ticket for the following evening's performance of 'The Magic Flute' at the Moscow Chamber Opera Theatre and a plain white card with a brief note for the reader:

'Be at the theatre tomorrow night. Remember to wear your overcoat and hat.'

The Colonel finished reading the note. He'd soon be in the West with a new identity and a new life. He pocketed the note and the ticket, folded the newspaper and headed for his office. He had one final task to do – call Lufthansa to arrange his flight to Frankfurt – which would cause alarm bells to ring loudly in the ears of anyone listening in on the conversation. The Colonel chuckled to himself as he walked.

CHAPTER 16

Andy used much of the next day in the safe house to pack Tex's belongings away. He'd underestimated how much Tex had brought with him, and accumulated, over the few short months he'd lived at the apartment. By the time he'd finished it was nearly three in the afternoon. He'd skipped lunch as he was keen to clear the apartment before the end of the day.

Whilst it served a practical purpose, Andy realised the packing kept his mind occupied as the clock ticked slowly down to the zero hour at eight. With the packing over, he made himself a cheese and pickle sandwich and allowed his mind to work through the plan, for the umpteenth time, again. Naturally, doubt and uncertainty seeped in.

What if the ticket had been found under the bench? What if The Colonel didn't follow the instructions? What if Malchik was one step ahead and had detained The Colonel? What if the plan doesn't work? The 'what ifs' kept coming. An obscure thought crossed his mind, *if the plan fails, no one in Langley would know of its failure.* He was insulated, the only loser, apart from The Colonel, would be Jack Masters at the FBI.

With his sandwich finished and his mood much improved, Andy needed to call in a favour so he grabbed his jacket and headed out of the door.

***

Vladim smiled when Andy entered his office; moments earlier he'd had the look of a haunted man. He stood and shook Andy's hand enthusiastically. "Hello, what brings you here?" Vladim asked.

"I came looking for you. But first, how are you? What's happening with Popov?"

"As you see, I'm still here!" Vladim shrugged. "I paid Popov what I thought I owed," his expression changed, he looked pained, "but ... he increased the amount again. The swine won't leave me alone."

"What will you do?"

"Work harder and keep paying. That's all I can do," Vladim sounded resigned to his fate. "Now you my friend. What about you?"

"I'm fine. Popov and his men have been chasing me around town, but they need to get fitter and lose a few pounds."

Vladim laughed, then spoke, "He said I need to pay up or else. I wish I could outrun him, but he knows I'll be at my office."

"I'll see what I can do to help," Andy sounded sympathetic, but he couldn't tell whether Vladim believed him or not.

"So, why are you here?" Vladim asked as he reached into a drawer and removed a large bottle of vodka and two glasses. He placed them on his desk and started pouring.

"My car has had some, um ... problems, and I need someone to drive me around the city this evening."

Vladim slid one of the glasses towards Andy and held the other. "What happened to your car?"

"It caught fire. I believe it's a write-off."

45

"That's not good. Was it a cheap Russian car?"

"Something like that." Andy didn't want to say his car had been shot at too!

Vladim raised his glass to Andy. Andy copied Vladim. The two men clashed their glasses together with enthusiasm. Some of the clear liquid spilled out of Andy's glass. "To friendship."

"To friendship," Andy repeated, then drained his glass in a single swig. The cheap vodka burnt the back of his throat and after a second, slowly warmed his stomach. Vladim started to recharge their glasses.

"Where do you need to go?" Vladim asked as he picked up his glass and started to refill it.

Andy passed him his glass and said, "This is the last one for today," Vladim looked disappointed but he continued, "I have work to do. I need to be at the Moscow Chamber Opera Theatre before eight tonight. Would you be able to drive me?" Andy looked Vladim in the eyes. He badly needed his help with the plan this evening and hoped he wouldn't ask too many questions. Vladim paused, looked at his glass of vodka then looked directly at Andy.

"Of course, that's what friends do," he said as his eyes sparkled.

"Thank you. I'll try and make this up to you, somehow." Andy said raising his glass to meet Vladim's. "To good fortunes."

"To good fortunes," Vladim responded.

Both men knocked back their glasses and returned the empty glasses onto the table.

"We'll be out for a few hours. I hope that's okay?" Andy said.

"I hadn't planned anything for tonight. So I'm looking forward to your company." Vladim glanced at his watch. "We should go out for dinner. Let's eat early, otherwise we'll be hungry."

"Where do you recommend we eat?"

"I know a good Armenian place not far from here. They serve great Chi Kofte and their Baklava is the best in Moscow."

"My kind of food, let's go!" Andy said suddenly aware that he was hungry.

Chapter 17

The sudden jarring sound of the ringing phone disturbed Oleg Malchik from his deep thoughts as he read his team's weekly operational report on Colonel Shanina. Malchik picked up the phone. "What?" he asked abruptly.

"The Colonel has just booked return flights to Frankfurt leaving tonight at midnight," the voice on the far end informed.

Malchik smiled, so far Shanina had shown no signs of any changes to his routine, everything was normal, until now.

"Which airline? Is he travelling alone?" Malchik demanded, his voice couldn't hide his excitement. From the volumes of information his team had gathered on their target, there was no apparent reason for him to travel overseas, this was the break they were looking for, *maybe the traitor is finally making his move.*

"He's on Lufthansa. Travelling alone."

Why now? Malchik thought as he rubbed his chin. *The death of the American spy could have made him nervous, maybe even tip him over the edge, and he's decided to run. The fool!* "Are there any other persons of interest on the same flight?" he asked while his mind spun quickly. *Who are your minders? Is it the Americans? They would normally have eyes on the same flight to watch and keep their mark calm.*

"No one on our database at present."

Somehow, Shanina would have help, his handlers would be fools to let him travel alone. "Are there any Americans on the same flight?" As he waited for the answer he finished the last of the cold, sweet coffee sitting on his desk.

"There are two Americans."

This information had Malchik sit up straight in his seat, *ah ha, got you!* "Tell me more."

"Two men. Blake Bolton, aged fifty-six, and Gary Mentor, aged sixty-four," the voice replied, "it says they are pastors from Ohio."

"Interesting, have either of them been in Russia previously? How long have they been here on this trip?" Another long pause followed. Malchik was pleased Shanina had made his move. His team would add a little pressure, make him uncomfortable, then detain him, and the two Americans, as they boarded their flight.

"This is Bolton's first time in Russia; Mentor has been here five times. They have been in Russia for six days. They flew together from Frankfurt to Saint Petersburg and, three days ago, flew from Saint Petersburg to Moscow."

This could be it: Shanina's extraction team posing as men of religion. Malchik felt good. Another traitor taken down by him would help further his career, he smiled, "Good work. Get the team assembled. Five minutes in the briefing room. I want the treacherous dog to feel some heat."

***

The Colonel could sense them watching him long before he saw them. Seated on a metal bench across from the entrance to his office building, a middle aged woman, wearing a green dress and grey jacket, her hair worn up in a tight bun. She looked out of place pretending to read a magazine using the light cast by a nearby lamppost.

One.

He turned right out of the building on his usual route home as he headed for the Metro. He spotted two more on the other side of the road. He noticed the men had been loitering until he stepped out of the building, the next moment they were walking with purpose in the same direction as him.

Two and Three.

As the Colonel turned right two blocks along he paused, as if he had suddenly remembered something, and glanced back. The tail had little chance to avoid being seen by the Colonel.

Four.

Two young men wearing leather jackets and blue jeans climbed out of an official looking car parked opposite the Metro. He watched as the car pulled away. The men crossed the road and fell in behind him as he descended the steps into the Metro.

Five and Six.

He couldn't be certain whether the young couple at the bottom of the escalator, seemingly in a romantic embrace, were watching him or whether his paranoia was growing.

CHAPTER 18

Although he'd lived in Moscow for many years, Colonel Shanina had never been to the Opera theatre. He'd driven and walked past it many times, but he'd not been through its doors. He needed to take his mind from the surveillance teams following him. He'd identified four more on the route from his apartment and he suspected there were more. Inside the theatre foyer he weaved his way through the crowd of opera lovers and headed for the doors leading to the stalls, showing his ticket to a nearby attendant.

The door on the left, your seat is at the front by the orchestra pit," the attendant smiled and moved on to assist the next theatregoer. The Colonel turned and caught a glimpse of two of his shadows pushing their way to the front of the queue at the ticket booth. Another agent, located to the right of the main entrance, failed to use his hand-held radio discretely, making him easy to spot.

The Colonel entered the main theatre and headed down the left side of the auditorium to take his seat at the front. As per his instructions, he'd dressed in his long overcoat and wore his hat. With the performance only minutes from starting, the Colonel found his seat and unbuttoned his coat slightly. He knew the theatre would become uncomfortably warm, however, his instructions were clear.

'Keep your overcoat and hat on during the performance.'

The sound of a solo oboe playing a single note, strong and steady, was joined swiftly by the other instruments building the crescendo to a forte of discordant notes as the orchestra tuned-up. Less than a minute later the orchestra fell silent.

The lights dimmed, then for a moment, they went out completely plunging the theatre into darkness. The lights flickered and came back on, this time dimmed to their performance level. The stage was now illuminated ready for the actors as the orchestra began the prelude to part one. The Colonel looked over his shoulder and saw four men rushing towards him. His heart raced and he closed his eyes. *This was it. They're going to take me into custody.*

He waited for what seemed an age expecting to feel eager hands grab him by the collar and drag him from his seat. Several seconds passed and nothing happened. He opened his eyes and, to his surprise, he saw the agents walking away. He realized he'd been holding his breath and, relieved he wasn't under arrest, he started to breath easily again and turned his attention back to the stage.

The Colonel enjoyed the first-half as best as he could, knowing that, at any moment, they could arrest him. When the production reached the interval and the music stopped, the lights flickered for a few seconds before they came back on. The noise from the audience increased as they stood to stretch legs, use the restrooms or purchase ice creams and drinks. The Colonel remained seated continuing to play his part as instructed even though he felt uncomfortably warm in his heavy clothing. He could feel several pairs of eyes watching from around the theatre, but when he looked, they averted their gaze and didn't make eye contact.

After ten minutes the bell rang to indicate that the part-two would be commencing shortly. With the audience back in their seats the lights flickered and went out. Once again the theatre was plunged back into darkness, a few moments later, the lights in the theatre flickered on, dimmed low and the orchestra enthusiastically introduced the second-half of the opera.

***

Standing across the street from the theatre, watching restlessly, was Malchik. He saw the lights go off and demanded an immediate update on his radio. He paced anxiously along the sidewalk when, a few seconds later, the theatre lights came back on. *Shitty wiring! They need to get it fixed. Next thing the place will burn down.* he thought just as his radio came to life and a voice gave him the information he wanted to hear.

"Sir, the Colonel is still seated in the same place, he hasn't moved."

"Keep watching. Only detain him if he makes any sudden moves, otherwise, we'll pick him up as planned." Malchik smiled, he had one team here at the theatre and another waiting at the airport for the pick-up. A third had eyes on Bolton and Mentor. He could sense the successful outcome of the mission was near and soon he'd be making the biggest arrest of his career so far.

He wasn't sure what made him turn, but when he did, he saw an old grey Volvo driving down the road away from the theatre. In the passenger seat he caught a fleeting glimpse of someone resembling the dead CIA agent; he knew this was impossible as he had witnessed Flint being permanently 'retired' from service. Still, the feeling something wasn't quite right had him reaching for his notepad. In the circumstances, with so much at stake, why change the habit of a lifetime? He made a note of the Volvo's registration plate as it stopped briefly at a set of traffic lights.

I'll have it checked later ... once we have Shanina in custody.

CHAPTER 19

Can you drop my friend off? He's in a hurry," Andy asked Vladim.

Sure, where do we need to go?" After receiving his instructions Vladim drove through the quiet Moscow streets. He knew from the edginess of his new passenger, and how he quickly hid in the back of his car, now wasn't the time to ask too many questions.

Vladim pulled into a convenient side street close to the stranger's destination and stopped. He continued to look out of the front windscreen while the man climbed from the back. As the stranger climbed out of the car, he paused briefly and thanked Vladim who simply nodded his head. Andy was already out of the car and shook the stranger's hand. "Good luck," he said.

Thank you. I'll need it," replied the stranger. His voice couldn't mask his nervousness. It looked like he wanted to say something else, but instead he turned and quickly strode confidently away. Andy walked around the corner of the side street and watched as The Colonel bound up the stairs and into the building without giving as much as a backward glance. Andy re-joined Vladim in the car.

What the was that about?" Vladim asked.

He's a man with problems and I'm just helping him out." Andy's answer had an element of truth, but he was careful not to give too much away so as to protect both The Colonel and Vladim. An awkward silence fell between them as Vladim drove back towards his office. Andy was first to break the silence.

Could you drop me off near the US Embassy?"

Is that where you work?" Vladim's pitch had risen and his volume raised a notch or two.

Yes."

What have you got me mixed up in?"

Best not to know just in case things don't work out. Can you drop me off? I'll make it worth your while." The awkward silence returned as Vladim drove Andy towards the Embassy. Once Andy was out of the car, Vladim sped away without saying another word, leaving a cloud of dark oily smoke in his wake.

***

Vladim parked in the garage and made his way up to his office. He'd decided to head to the office rather than inflict his bad mood on his mother, father and sister. Vladim wanted his business to be a success so he could afford to buy his own place to live and maybe, if he was lucky, somewhere for his sister too.

His heart sank when he found the office door open and the lights on. Sat in the reception area was Ivan and one of his thugs. Ivan looked at Vladim, the other continued to entertain himself by spinning around on an office swivel chair.

Mr Popov wants to see you, in his office at the back," Ivan informed him indicating with his head the direction of Vladim's office. The spinning thug stopped himself, stood and dropped in behind Ivan who followed Vladim as he slowly made his way towards his office.

Popov was inside, sat with his feet resting on Vladim's desk while smoking a cigarette. He smiled, as Vladim entered, though his smile didn't reach his eyes which were cold and cruel. He stubbed the cigarette out on Vladim's desk.

"What do I have to do to make you understand?" Popov said as he took his feet off the desk and stood up.

"I don't know what you mean," Vladim protested.

Popov walked around the table and stood only inches from Vladim's face, "Every time I try and drive you out of business ... you keep paying up!"

Vladim didn't see the punch, but he felt its full force as it found its mark in his abdomen knocking the wind out of him. He bent double with pain and struggled to breathe. Popov casually searched through Vladim's jacket pockets and removed his wallet which he tossed to Ivan. Vladim couldn't breathe let alone put up any resistance to the search. Next, Popov stuffed his hands into Vladim's trouser pockets and felt his car keys being lifted.

"No. Not my car!" Vladim managed to gasp as, finally, some air made it into his lungs.

Popov threw the keys to the other thug who caught them with his right hand.

"Add it to my fleet," he instructed. Popov stepped away from Vladim and nodded to Ivan who'd just pocketed Vladim's wallet. This time Vladim saw the right hook but he didn't have time to react as the large fist struck him on the jaw knocking him to the floor. He tasted blood in his mouth and while he didn't see the follow up kick to his ribs he felt the intense pain it delivered.

"Ivan, take him to the basement and have some fun with him," Popov laughed.

Firm hands grabbed Vladim, dragged him out of his office and down the corridor towards the stairs where both thugs set about beating him. Vladim hoped the beating would stop as kicks rained down on him, striking his arms, legs, back and head. The thugs stopped their assault long enough to drag him down the concrete stairs to the basement. Through his swollen eyes he could see a metal chair and four more thugs waiting for him under the light of a single dull lightbulb.

This is going to hurt. He wondered whether he would make it out alive as the blows kept coming; then everything went black as he slipped into unconsciousness while the thugs continued their assault on his broken body.

he last notes of the performance faded out and once the enthusiastic applause from the audience ad died down, the lights flickered again before lighting up the main theatre. The hubbub from the udience increased as people talked appreciatively about the show as they started to file out.

utside the theatre, Malchik watched as the first of the audience spilled out onto the sidewalk. His adio crackled to life.

Sir? You need to come inside."

his wasn't a message he expected to hear. He held the radio up and spoke into it, "What's the roblem?"

Sir, you need to come inside and see," the voice sounding just a little bit too urgent for comfort.

Malchik ran towards the entrance. "Get out of the way. Make way!" he shouted as he fought against he tide of exiting crowd. A gap cleared allowing him to enter the building. One of his team met him nd led him into the main auditorium. The agent directed Malchik's attention to a man sitting in the ront row wearing a heavy coat and hat. From their position it looked like Colonel Shanina, but unlike he other members of the audience, this man remained seated.

Was that Shanina's seat?" Malchik demanded.

Yes, Sir, but I don't think it's him."

he man wearing the hat stood and slowly turned to make his way to the exit.

Who the hell is that?" Malchik demanded, but before the agent could answer, Malchik strode past im bearing down on the man at the front of the auditorium. "You. Stay there!" Malchik ordered. he man stopped and waited for Malchik to join him. "You're under arrest," Malchik calmly informed he individual even though he was inwardly seething at the deception. "Now, who are you?"

he man smiled, removed his hat and addressed Malchik: "I'm Ambassador Rushbrooke of the nited States Government and I have full diplomatic immunity, so, no, I'm not under arrest."

Malchik turned away from the Ambassador.

Seal the theatre," Malchik ordered his men, "Now!" He turned back to face the Ambassador.

I'll be leaving with my wife; she should be on her way back from the restroom. Please make sure our people don't delay us further, my car will be outside waiting for us," the Ambassador said as he alked past the furious Malchik.

The Ambassador's party will be leaving the building shortly," Malchik hissed into the radio, "no one lse in or out."

Malchik turned to his subordinate, "Kindly escort our guests safely out of the building."

he Ambassador and his wife left the theatre, escorted by one of Malchik's underlings, climbed into heir official car and were soon on their way. The theatre swarmed with FSB officers whilst outside he local militia surrounded the building and stopped attendees from leaving. They doubted their arget was still inside the theatre so they extended their cordon and randomly stopped cars and men the street, checking their identity papers.

Malchik was working hard to maintain his composure as he thumbed through his notebook looking for some breadcrumbs to work with. He stopped at a page and paused for a second. *The Grey Volvo? Of course!*

He raised his radio and spoke into it with icy coolness. "Control, this is Oleg Malchik, run the following number plate for me," he read the Volvo's registration number as he headed for the exit. He didn't have time to stand idly waiting for the information. He was certain the Volvo was the breadcrumb he needed to solve Shanina's 'disappearance' and, if not, he still had one more opportunity to arrest Shanina ... at the airport.

By the time Malchik received details of the address he was on the sidewalk outside the theatre. He looked at his watch and thought about timings. Malchik made up his mind. He ordered his men to get into their cars ready to follow him to the address and requested police units to meet them there. Raiding the address could yield more important clues or, if they were lucky, deliver Shanina on a plate. Moments later Malchik sat in the lead car feeling confident that his quarry was within his grasp.

CHAPTER 21

Popov's thug, Ivan, used a rope to tie his unconscious victim's feet and hands together and around a chair he had placed in the basement, pulling the rope tight to make sure his victim wasn't going anywhere. When he was satisfied the knots would hold, he stood back and threw a bucket of cold water over his victim to bring him round … then Ivan and his friends continued their assault.

Their victim screamed with pain as the blows and kicks rained down on him. The thugs were happy in their work knowing the sounds of their brutality wouldn't carry beyond the thick walls of the basement. Their victim knew if anyone did hear it, they wouldn't report it, or they would be sitting in the chair instead of him. The beating continued, unrelenting, until Ivan held up his hand.

"Let's take a break. I need some refreshment, so let's get a few beers," he suggested. The others nodded their approval as the basement was warm and their exertion had made them thirsty. He held up the keys to the Volvo: "Look, our friend here has kindly given us his car!" he said before laughing out loud, the rest of the thugs joined in as they made their way up the stairs leaving their unfortunate victim broken and alone.

The five large men grumbled as they squeezed themselves into the Volvo. Ivan put the key in the ignition and the engine came to life. He pulled out onto the quiet main road towards the bottle store where they had an 'account' courtesy of Popov's protection scheme. They weren't sure what happened next but two police cars suddenly appeared in front of them and blocked their path causing Ivan to slam his foot on the brake to prevent a collision. Panicked, Ivan put the car in reverse in an attempt to escape only to find two more police cars had pulled up behind and hemmed them in. They were stuck, uncomfortably crammed in the car, with policemen running towards them from all directions; weapons drawn. There was no way out.

A man in civilian clothes opened the driver's door and pointed a large pistol at Ivan's head. The cold steel from the tip of the barrel pressed into his skin, this close, he could see the pistol's hammer had been cocked, Ivan automatically raised his hands to indicate he wasn't armed or going to resist.

"Don't shoot! Don't shoot!" Ivan pleaded. There was no reply just an indication to get out of the car which he did, slowly, making sure he didn't make any sudden moves that would give the pistol's owner an excuse to squeeze the trigger. The rest of the thugs were dragged from the Volvo and joined Ivan lying face down on the road. Moments later they were all handcuffed.

Malchik stepped forward and squatted down close to Ivan: "You're in so much shit, who else is involved with this?" he demanded, "be careful how you answer this as my patience is running very thin."

Ivan struggled to get his words out, partly because he was finding it hard to breath and partly because he was afraid, very afraid. Since Popov had recruited him, he was usually the one with the gun and holding a hapless victim down on the ground, but now he was on the receiving end. "Upstairs! Upstairs in the office! He's in the office! On the third floor!" Ivan curled round as much as he could to indicate the building they'd just come from.

Malchik stood up and quickly set off on foot to the building's entrance followed by three of his team. His pistol swung in his right hand as he ran up the stairs, easily clearing two steps at a time. He paused by the dark green door. This was the Volvo's registered address. The FSB officers formed up behind him ready to go in.

Malchik used the fingers on his left hand to count down from three. They burst into the office quickly clearing the empty rooms. Making their way through the large workshop to reach the back office they were approached by a short man wearing an ill-fitting suit waving a gun at them.

"What the bloody hell are you doing in my office?" the man bellowed at the FSB officers.

Malchik saw the gun, raised his own and without any hesitation fired. As the man fell to the floor he dropped his pistol and clutched his chest, moaning with pain. Malchik watched as a trail of dark blood started to grow and pool on the carpet around the man. "Get an ambulance!" Malchik instructed one of his team as he knelt by Popov: "Where is he?" Malchik demanded, his voice low and menacing. The man's breathing was shallow and rapid which made it difficult to suck in the air he needed to stay alive. Malchik had no intention of getting blood over his hands so made no effort to plug the man's large chest wound, instead he repeated the question: "Where is he?"

As blood trickled slowly out of the corner of his mouth, Popov managed to gasp what would be his last words: "Downstairs. The basement. I'm sorry." Popov struggled to stay conscious as his life ebbed away. Malchik stood and moved towards the door: "You, stay here," he ordered the closest agent, "the rest of you, follow me."

Malchik ran back to the corridor and headed for the stairwell. He felt excited as he ran down the stairs to the basement believing his quarry was almost within his grasp. He reached the drab green steel door to the basement and turned the handle then pushed hard to open the door. He saw only darkness. *Damn!* He blindly felt around the doorway for the light switch, *"there you are..."* he muttered to himself as he flicked the small switch down.

A dull light filled the large room revealing a lone figure tied to a chair. Malchik's heart raced. He had his man. He strode forward confidently with his team following closely behind. He reached the slumped figure, grabbed the man's hair with his left hand and yanked his head upright.

"Thank God you're here!" murmured the victim.

"Who the hell are you?" Malchik demanded.

Chapter 22

Malchik and his team of FSB agents drove at high speed through the city streets to reach Sheremetyevo Alexander Pushkin International Airport to join the team already in position. They conducted their journey in silence as Malchik, quietly seething, remained deep in his private thoughts going over and over the evening's events minute by minute. *That cunning fox, Shanina, must have somehow used the Volvo and the man tied up in the basement as a distraction to buy time.* Malchik was annoyed with himself at falling for the trick and not remaining focused on the airport and the late night flight to Frankfurt.

As Malchik leapt out the car his radio came to life: "Bolton and Mentor are airside and located in the Irish bar, Sir."

"Anyone with them?" Malchik asked as he ran through the terminal.

"No, sir," came the reply.

Malchik glanced at his watch as he entered the terminal building his eyes darted around looking for Shanina. He raised his radio to speak. "Has Shanina got his boarding pass yet?"

"No, sir."

He's cutting it fine to catch his midnight flight out. He'll have to arrive in the next few minutes or the desk won't issue his boarding pass. Malchik slowed to a walk heading in the direction of the Lufthansa check-in desks, sweat dripping down the sides of his face from his exertion and the excitement of the chase.

"Sir, a tall man wearing a woollen suit, large overcoat and hat, has just walked in from the other entrance.'

He must have evaded them by entering the building from the Arrivals Hall. "Where is he?" Malchik looked around, scanning faces. He was still quite a distance from the Lufthansa desks. He picked up his speed to a slow jog and soon arrived at the first check-in desk.

"Approaching desk sixty-eight, Sir," came the reply.

"Are you sure it's him?" Malchik asked looking up to see which desk he was passing. *Desk twenty-seven ... I'm not going to be there in time to arrest him in person.* With the disappointment palpable he started to run; he wasn't going to be late at this party!

"No, Sir, there are too many people and I can't be sure but he appears to fit the description."

"What's he doing now?"

"He's at the Business Class desk check-in."

Malchik looked up. *Desk forty-eight. Come on!*

"Have we got people near the desk?" Malchik asked.

"Yes, Sir."

"Stall him at the desk. I want to be there when we move in."

"Yes, Sir."

Less than thirty seconds later Malchik could see desk sixty-eight with its Lufthansa logo and sign: 'Business Class Check-in'.

Through the crowd he saw the back of a tall man wearing a heavy coat and hat standing at the desk. Two of his agents were either side of him, while another stood behind the check-in desk with the airline representative and held the man's passport. Malchik got closer and looked at the agent holding the passport, his face said it all as the agent looked up to see Malchik and shook his head.

It's got to be him. Malchik reached the counter and his team.

"Sir, this is Hans Schmidt," the agent holding the passport informed him.

Malchik felt the knot in his stomach tighten. His day had gone from bad to worse.

"Take your hat off and face me!" Malchik demanded. The man removed his hat and faced Malchik. Aside from being taller than average, and well dressed, he bore only a passing resemblance to Shanina. It was all he could do to keep a lid on his temper and, as calmly as possible, he apologised for the delay and informed Schmidt he could carry on with his journey. The agent returned his passport as the airline representative handed him his boarding pass.

The agent turned to Malchik: "What do we do now, Sir?"

CHAPTER 23

The first rays of daylight started to break through the grey mist which blanketed the port facility. The display on his digital watch read six fifty-three. With the temperature just a few degrees above zero Shanina fastened his heavy coat to protect him from the early morning chill. He was pleased he had his hat to keep his head warm.

Shanina walked into the security office at the entrance to the port and flashed his FSB credentials at one of the two guards who sat looking bored. The office lacked signs of maintenance as the yellow paint peeled from the walls and some of the office lights were broken. Shanina cast his gaze around the room and thought the guards were lazy judging by the discarded take-out food cartons which littered the desks. He didn't want to remain in here for too long as the room was filled with the stale smell of tobacco and body odour.

After a cursory glance at his papers, they gave the Colonel directions to Building Twelve, the 'Ports and Aerodrome' office. The security guards knew Building Twelve to be an FSB outpost and had been briefed not to ask questions about what went on there. Shanina was soon on his way towards Building Twelve knowing Boris Nevich would be on duty and expecting him.

Through the early morning mist Shanina could make out the silhouettes of two large container ships and a P&O cruise liner berthed at the wharfs. Two large cranes moved across the container ships plucking metal containers off the ships and carefully placing them on port transporters which effortlessly shuttled them between the ships and the holding area for customs clearance and onward despatch out of the port.

By the time Shanina reached Building Twelve, daylight had broken through the mist and he could see more of the hustle and bustle of the busy facility. Shanina didn't bother to knock, he opened the grey wooden door and walked straight in. Facing Shanina was a uniformed FSB officer walking from the kitchen towards the main office, he held a coffee cup in his right hand and a thick slice of black bread smeared with butter in his left. The FSB officer stopped when he saw the visitor.

"Who are you?" he demanded, he clearly wasn't expecting a visitor this early in the morning; especially one who thought he could enter a restricted area without an invitation.

The Colonel smiled benevolently: "I'm Colonel Shanina from Moscow. Boris Nevich is expecting me. Please be kind enough to show me to his office."

The officer nodded briefly and indicated that Shanina should follow him. They walked through an open doorway into a spacious office which had four desks and two computers with bulky CRT screens. A large printer sat on the edge of a table. Two uniformed FSB officers, sat behind their desks, looked up from their paperwork as Shanina and the third officer entered.

"Boris Nevich?" Shanina asked the two seated officers.

The bald officer stood looking sheepish.

"That's me, are you Colonel Shanina?" he asked.

Shanina faced the approaching officer who looked to be in his early thirties. Even through his drab uniform Shanina could tell the officer worked out regularly. "Yes. I'm here as part of Operation Octagon. You should have received the briefing note and your instructions from Yuri Stepanov in Moscow."

Octagon had been Shanina's own creation and he'd sent the briefing note easily forging Stepanov's signature which told Nevich to facilitate an officer gaining passage on a container ship as part of a covert infiltration operation. That and the legitimate order to provide the visiting senior officer with their full co-operation should have been enough to convince Nevich to assist.

Nevich gave Shanina's hand a firm shake and looked directly at him eye-to-eye as he said, "We don't receive many visitors from Moscow. This must be special." Shanina felt uncomfortable as Nevich maintained his gaze, doubts started creeping into his mind. *Did Nevich smell a rat? Did he know the first signal didn't come from Stepanov?*

"Let me tell Yuri you've arrived safely, and we'll then proceed with your operation." Nevich said as he returned to his desk.

Damn! I didn't plan for this. "No, it's okay. There's no time as the operation is underway." Shanina said in an attempt to stall the officer.

"I'm not stupid. I won't say anything which compromises your operation," Nevich replied as he picked up his phone and dialled a number from memory. The room became unusually warm; Shanina started to sweat. Nevich listened as the phone in Stepanov's office rang without answer. He hung up and immediately dialled another number. "There'll be someone in the main office," he said confidently.

Shanina turned away and wiped his brow with his hand, then wiped his hand on the back of his overcoat. With his brow clear of sweat, Shanina faced Nevich who now looked puzzled as his second call went unanswered. "Maybe they're busy or been called away to a meeting. I have lots of meetings in Moscow," Shanina said as he shrugged his shoulders.

Nevich stayed on the line for another ten seconds then hung up: "Stepanov is normally at his desk early. I'll call again later, I'm sure he will want to know we've been helpful." Nevich stood from his desk and approached the Colonel before continuing, "you have a cabin on the '*Mykonos*' bound for Rotterdam, it leaves at high tide in an hour, so we have to move quickly to get you on-board."

"Good, I don't want any further delays," Shanina replied, "a lot of work has gone into this operation, it would be a disappointment if we don't get a result!"

CHAPTER 24

Malchik read the report for the third time, looking for the lie. The facts as presented were simple enough to understand:

> The car used by the unknown CIA Agent to get away after the archives break-in resembled the Volvo registered to Vladimir Martirossian. During the escape the car had been fired on by one of the officers giving chase. Close examination of the Volvo registered to Vladimir Martirossian shows gunshot damage to the rear of the Volvo.

> The Volvo had been sighted at the Opera Theatre shortly after the performance interval and before Colonel Shanina's disappearance was discovered. Later that evening, when we stopped the Volvo in question, it contained five men all known to the police. They were arrested at the scene but, as yet, have not indicated they had any involvement in the archives breach or Colonel Shanina's disappearance.

> On entering the business address of Vladimir Martirossian, we were approached by Maximillian Popov. Popov was also known to the police due to his long criminal history and alleged criminal activities. Popov approached us in an aggressive manner while brandishing a loaded firearm. I was concerned for our safety and fired a single round to neutralise the threat. Popov died at the scene as a result of his injuries.

> We searched the area and found Vladimir Martirossian tied to a chair in the building's basement. Martirossian had been badly beaten; it was clear he could not have tied himself to the chair. The medical examination of Martirossian concluded his injuries had been sustained over a period of a few days as new injuries had been inflicted upon older wounds which had yet to heal.

> While being interviewed in hospital, Martirossian claimed that he'd had problems with Popov going back many months. Martirossian said that a few days ago, matters escalated when he was abducted, his wallet and car keys taken, and he had been tied to the chair in the basement where he had been beaten repeatedly by Popov's men; he could not say what Popov's men had been doing with his car in the days since his abduction. Despite being the registered owner of the Volvo, it would appear that the presence of Vladimir Martirossian was coincidental; Martirossian is not linked to Popov's criminal activity and, therefore, no longer a person of interest.

> We recovered a large amount of foreign currency, which came to twenty thousand US dollars. This was found in a leather bag, in the office that Popov emerged from prior to being shot. The fingerprints on the bag match the fingerprints of the unknown CIA Agent found at the archives following the breach. This confirms our suspicions that Popov was paid for his services by the American Government.

> In conclusion, it would appear that Popov was using Martirossian's address to mask his criminal activities. Popov was also colluding with the Americans by assisting the security breach at the archives and the disappearance of Colonel Shanina at the theatre. It would appear that Popov was acting alone and, following his death, our line of investigation is now closed.

Malchik put the file down and with both hands rubbed his temples to ease the stress he felt. He picked up the phone and called his team monitoring Martirossian's bedside. They answered within three rings.

"Hello?"

"This is Malchik."

"Sir?" the voice on the distant end replied.

"You can stand down. He's not of interest to us."

"Yes, Sir, understood," the line went dead.

Just as Malchik replaced the receiver in its cradle, there was a knock on his office door, and before he could issue his usual curt response, the door opened and General Dudek's Staff Officer, walked in "General Dudek has summoned you. Come with me."

Malchik had taken the unusual step of wearing his uniform as he'd expected the call from 'upstairs'. Following the General's Staff Officer out of his office towards the elevators, Malchik could feel the stares of the people gathered in the main office area. He made no attempt to make eye contact, just focussed straight ahead, as he walked towards his punishment for failing to arrest Colonel Shanina, prevent him from leaving Russia and allowing him to defect to the Americans. He knew he had allowed his previous successes to impact on his handling of Shanina and, instead of his usual calculated direct action, had given his target just enough room to wriggle free. He deserved to be held to account, as he would expect nothing less from his chain of command.

General Dudek didn't look up from his paperwork as his Staff Officer ushered Malchik into his office. Malchik came to a halt in front of the General's desk, saluted and remained at attention, looking straight ahead: "Lieutenant Malchik reporting, Sir."

Malchik noticed his voice had developed a slight tremble. Dudek was a legend within the FSB, a thirty-year veteran who had known Krushchev and reported directly to Brezhnev for his *special projects*. Dudek had the ear of the Politburo and Malchik had heard rumours that each General Secretary of the Communist Party would confide their secrets with Dudek and, in return, he would keep their secrets by removing any potential loose ends along the way. Dudek knew where the bodies were buried which wasn't difficult ... he'd put most of them there!

After several seconds Dudek looked up, his piercing dark eyes bore into Malchik's soul. Malchik couldn't help but notice a scar which ran across Dudek's throat as though someone had once tried to garrotte him.

"Malchik. What am I to do with you?" Dudek asked. Malchik remained standing at attention, his mouth firmly closed. "You have created a diplomatic incident with America by killing a CIA agent on Russian soil, the wrong agent from all accounts, and trying to arrest the US Ambassador, in public, or a night at the theatre with his wife. Finally, and most importantly, you had a traitor, who was about to defect, under close surveillance and, with over twenty agents at your disposal, you allowed him to escape. Have you any idea of how much your ineptness will damage our operations both here and overseas?"

Malchik felt the room closing in on him. His chest tightened. He couldn't speak ... it didn't matter he wasn't expected to respond ... he just had to take the hit ... his previous successes counted for nothing at this exact moment ... the General's decision would be final and his career stopped in its tracks ... or worse!

"Do I have you serve twenty-five years of hard labour or taken outside and shot?"

he light was starting to fade as the spectacular golden sunset was coming to an end. The elongated shadows from the New York skyscrapers were pointing further into the distance as the sun touched the horizon. Andy savoured the moment as he knew the shadows would soon be gone and the sun with them.

he refreshingly cool beer went down smoothly as the two men toasted The Colonel's good fortune. The Colonel had been debriefed day and night over the last three months and moved between safe houses each week, sometimes twice in a week, often with no notice. The rooftop bar overlooking New York's iconic skyline made an appropriate venue for The Colonel's first outing since his defection. Even so the FBI took no chances; three agents sat at the next table and two more covered the entrance.

oday was a special day – he'd been given his new identity, Karl Lentov – complete with his US citizenship and passport. Here, he was celebrating his new life and relative freedom. He smiled as he shared a cold beer with the CIA agent who made it happen.

Do you know what happened after you left?" Andy asked.

Only small bits, from here and there, naturally my former colleagues and friends don't return my calls." The two men laughed. Lentov continued, "Boris Nevich didn't talk with his boss Yuri Stepanov as Stepanov and his colleagues were all hungover from the vodka I'd left with them ... sometimes it pays to keep your head down and 'forget' you helped a 'traitor' escape!"

What of Malchik?" Andy asked.

entov took a sip of his beer and continued: "Malchik got posted to Novosibirsk for two years as a way to appease the Americans and for his failure to take me into custody earlier ... but he'll be back."

How do you know that?"

Dudek likes him. I think Malchik will go far in the FSB... his current posting is just a reminder of how quickly your fortune can change ... he won't be so easy to fool again!"

I'll bear that in mind ... next time!"

CHAPTER 26

Four months had gone quickly for Vladim and his fortunes had changed. The physical scars from his ordeal had healed, but the mental ones would take longer to fade. The canvas bag, waiting for him when he came out of hospital, contained fifty-thousand dollars in US dollar bills and had helped rebuild his life.

He relocated his business to a prime location one block from the central police station. His staff turned up to work without fear of being attacked. Vladim's business was growing and he'd just put down a sizeable deposit on an apartment he'd craved for himself many months ago. Finally, he traded in his old Volvo for a newer model which didn't belch oily smoke ... or have bullet holes as a decorative feature.

Sitting at his desk in his new office, he held a large glass of vodka and wondered whether he'd see Andy Flint again. Their chance encounter had changed his life: his staff were happy; his business was booming; and Max Popov, Ivan and his thugs would never bother him, or anyone else again.

Vladim held the glass up to the light and looked at the clear liquid, then, in one swift move, he downed its contents and slammed the glass onto the table. He jumped as he caught a glimpse of a figure standing in his doorway.

"Hello my old friend."

Vladim recognised the voice instantly. He smiled and reached for a second glass placing it on his desk next to his, filling them both to the brim ... this was going to be a long night.

**

CHAPTER 1

AUGUST 19

Andy shivered from the cold and pulled the zip'
he damp river air seeped through his clothin'
motor making the rigid inflatable boat accele.
he boat left in its wake worried him as it made him
ervous minutes Andy sped up river until the bright lights u.
low in the distance. A short time later the illuminated structure u
Andy eased the outboard motor down; the roar of the boat's engine fell u
nd slowed the inflatable down to a crawl. Andy looked behind, to his relief the
ut gone. *Okay so far,* he told himself.

The bright lights of the warehouse combined with the height of the wharf, created a long
hadow over the water which he exploited as he maneuvered the inflatable boat alongside
he wharf's ladder, precisely where he'd been told it would be. Andy cut the engine, slowing
the inflatable further as it pushed against the river's current then bumped against the
adder bringing the inflatable to a gentle stop. His heart quickened as he rushed forward and
used a black nylon rope to secure the boat against the ladder. With the boat secure, he
ripped the ladder with both gloved hands; the constant exposure to the river made its
ging metal slippery and tricky to get a firm grip. Tentatively, he pushed down on the first
ung with his right boot, it took his weight, and he slowly started to climb.

Reaching the top, he peered over the edge of the wharf and could see one of the external
ghts from the warehouse was broken. His confidence grew further – his asset had been
ight – the broken light formed a dark area around the only access door along this side of
he long structure. With his head above the side of the wharf, Andy carefully looked around
nd listened for signs of the guards he knew would be patrolling the area. He slowed his
breathing and hoped his heart rate would drop from racing to just pounding in his chest.

All looks clear, he told himself. His asset had said that – tonight – the side door would be
unlocked. He wrapped his right arm around the ladder and checked his watch … one–twelve
m. He remained in position as he watched the seconds tic away on his watch … one–
ourteen … *move!*

Andy climbed the last five rungs quickly, stepped onto the wharf and, without pausing, ran
owards the relative safety of the dark shadow covering the access door. With his back to
he structure, he checked his watch again … *the guards will be changing shifts about … now.*
He had less than five minutes to get in, find what he was looking for, gather evidence and
et out. It was not without risk; there remained a possibility he could be discovered by a
ecurity guard running late for the shift change.

Andy reached for the door ha
shoulder … the door crack
clear. Now or never! And
door open wide enoug
signalled the presenc
crouched down an
roof lights.

The warehous
the hushed
round he
slowly
muffl
As

65

ndle, pulled it down and gave it a gentle push with his
d open an inch. He peered inside the warehouse ... it was still
drew his silenced pistol from his shoulder holster and pushed the
for him to slip inside, quickly closing the door behind him (nothing
of an intruder more than an unexpected open door). He immediately
scanned the cavernous space lit by a dull yellow hew cast from the old

e seemed eerily quiet. There were no signs of movement, unusual noises or
voices of guards talking. *This is a bit odd, stay focused!* he told himself. Looking
could see a number of wooden crates in long rows stacked three high. Andy stood
nd, with his pistol raised, moved towards the nearest crate, his rubber-soled boots
g the sound of his footsteps.

he reached the first stack he put the pistol into his holster and, using both hands, opened
he lid of the top crate; inside were freshly minted assault rifles. Carefully closing the lid he
moved to the next stack of crates; this time, grenades ... Russian F1's. His asset had been
right: the arms shipment had arrived. Then, set slightly away from the others, a single crate
... *there you are!*

Andy approached the single crate and removed his small black backpack. He opened it and
removed a palm-sized digital camera, white cotton gloves, long thick black rubber gloves
and a military grade respirator. He made sure the three atropine injectors were easy to
reach by placing them on the floor by the crate ... even with the respirator and gloves he
was still at risk of nerve agent poisoning; the injectors were a *'fail safe'* and may just save his
life if exposed.

He slipped his hands into the cotton gloves before pulling on the thick black rubber pair up
to his elbows. He donned the respirator and pulled the straps which tighten the seal of the
mask against his face. His peripheral vision was restricted, but he'd rather have that
constraint than die an agonizing death within minutes of opening the crate.

His asset said the chemical shells and the arms shipment were headed for Saddam Hussein's
murderous regime in Iraq. Andy's orders from Langley were simple: gather evidence and
leave without being detected. His heart raced at the thought of getting this close to lethal
chemical munitions; one tiny drop would kill him. Andy felt nauseous and could feel the
sweat forming on his forehead and inside the respirator making the eyepieces fog up. He
closed his eyes, took three deep breaths, then, after a final look around (to check he was
still alone), he lifted the lid and looked inside the crate. *What the ... heck!* Andy was stunned
at what he saw.

The yellow radioactive hazard symbol wasn't what he expected. Andy looked down at the
objects and quickly realized they were nuclear tipped battlefield artillery shells. Desperate
for more clues he reached inside for the packing slip. The Russian writing on the paperwork
identified the consignment as 152mm 3BV3 nuclear shells and, according to the slip, they
were heading for Iraq. Andy's hands had a slight tremble as he took photos of the warheads

nd shipment paperwork. He replaced the paperwork, closed the lid and photographed the external marking on the crate.

Andy had a dilemma. Should he complete his mission and leave or stop nuclear weapons falling into the hands of Saddam Hussein? His mission had been based on information about chemical weapons. *Would my mission have been the same if Langley knew they were moving nuclear warheads?* he asked himself.

He removed the respirator and sucked in several deep breaths of damp air, then returned the respirator and camera to his backpack. Andy hesitated before removing the gloves but wearing them made it impossible for him to use his pistol so he didn't have much of a choice; death would be quick if he couldn't use his pistol and he wasn't ready to die … not today anyway! Andy took both pairs off and placed them all in his pack which he closed and secured. He checked his watch … one–nineteen. *I need to get out of here, I've got what I came for … no need for heroics*, he told himself, *but what about the warheads?*

He looked around and saw a pallet trolley by the wall of the warehouse. Andy cautiously made his way over to the trolley while constantly checking if anyone was around. He brought the trolley back and fed its two forks easily in the gaps underneath the pallet so he could raise it and pull it to the door … *Result!* … he felt pleased with himself … and that was when he heard the voices, two of them, and they were getting louder … *Shit!*

Andy abandoned the trolley and quickly moved to a darker area, squeezing between two tall pallets he became nearly invisible in between the lines of crates. He removed his pistol from its holster and held it steadily with his right hand, keeping it pointed at chest height. He felt a single bead of sweat slowly work its way down his forehead, right cheek then down onto his neck; his dry mouth added to his discomfort. Steadying his breath, he worked out there were two guards and listened to their conversation as they neared his hiding place.

Tomorrow all of this will be gone."

This is the third shipment this month. Why would the torch bearers send all of this to Iraq?"

Andy wasn't sure that he had caught what was being said … *Did he say lantern bearer, torch carrier, lantern carrier?* There were a number of different meanings to what he'd heard. A lack of accuracy would be a failure on his part.

It's always about the money."

The two men laughed as they walked away. Andy lowered his weapon, slowly squeezed out from his hiding space and looked around to check that the two guards had moved before committing himself to return to the trolley. Satisfied he was relatively safe, he tucked his pistol into its holster and headed to the door. To keep it open he applied a small wooden wedge which he found to the right of the door.

Andy struggled as he pulled the trolley outside. With thirty meters of open ground and a ladder to reach his boat, he felt both exposed and vulnerable. Andy removed the wedge and closed the door then looked around and listened for a few seconds. Nothing caught his attention, the only sounds he could hear were the gentle hum from the warehouse exterior lights and the low rumble of the moving water from the river. The coast looked clear.

Time to go, he whispered quietly to himself.

The weight of the munitions in the crate made moving the trolley over the open ground hard work. Even though the night air was just above freezing he could feel perspiration forming under his arms and beads of sweat on his forehead. Less than a minute later he was standing next to the ladder looking down at his inflatable boat four meters below.

His dilemma returned: leave the shells behind or find some way of taking them with him. He didn't want to leave the shells but his options were limited to ... none! *There's no way I can get the shells into the boat*, Andy admitted to himself. He knew he didn't have the strength and dexterity to carry the shells down to the boat one by one – the wharf ladder was way too slippery – and dropping them from this height would more than likely sink it. *I'll just have to ditch them and hope the water does the rest*, he decided.

Andy hauled the trolley a few meters further forward until he judged it was clear of his boat then pushed the crate with all his strength so that it toppled into the deep water below. The loud splash, as it hit the water, was amplified by the stillness of the night. *Damn!* Andy looked down to see the crate sink as the dark water quickly consumed it ... *time to move ...* but he had paused for a second too long, as he stood up to climb onto the ladder and start his descent into the safety of the shadows, he heard someone shout loudly behind him.

"Hey, you!"

Whoever it was wasn't waiting for a reply; Andy heard the eruption of gunfire and then the crack of a bullet as it passed close overhead. *Good job they aren't a good shot!* Andy moved quickly onto the ladder and slid down it without using the rungs. As he reached the bottom he slowed his descent and neatly stepped off the last rung of the ladder into the boat. He knew he'd bought himself precious seconds and, under the cover of the wharf he was safe, but now 'they' were closing in on his position above. *I need to get out of here ... pronto*, he told himself.

Andy untied the boat, moved to the rear of the inflatable and pulled the rip-start on the engine – nothing happened – he opened the choke and pulled the rip-start again. The sixty-horsepower engine made no effort to start. *Shit! Not now!* He pulled the rip-start again ... still nothing ... *this isn't good ...* his heart was racing. He could hear the shouts getting closer if he didn't move quickly they would be right on top of him.

Andy tried to think back to his training at the Farm when they'd had a session on small boat handling, then he remembered what to do and quickly applied three firm squeezes to the fuel bulb. *Now would be good*, he thought as he pulled the rip-start again. The engine turned ... it didn't fire but it had made an effort and that was progress! His arms were starting to ache, "Come on!" he shouted at the stubborn outboard engine ... *I don't want to have to swim!*

He gave the rip-start one last chance and pulled hard; he really didn't want to have to swim. The engine fired and roared to life. *Yes!* Andy pulled the gear lever towards him and twisted the grip sending the inflatable forwards rapidly along the side of the wharf. *The longer I can use the wharf for cover the better*. When he reached the end of the wharf, where the river narrowed, Andy turned the inflatable in a large arc to get as close as possible to the far river bank.

The lights from the warehouse illuminated him as he drove the boat hard and fast down the river. The white wash from the boat's wake made him easier to spot, but all he cared about was getting away. The air lit up with lines of red tracer which zipped angrily around him and, then, the water started to dance as the rounds that followed missed their intended target ... him! It felt like minutes, but could only have been seconds, before he was finally out of the glare of the warehouse lights and into the darkness. He felt relief wash over him as he reached the bend in the river and safety from the gunfire.

He's an alcoholic, no job, unable to pay his bills and has a date with a judge. Now there's an SUV with government plates watching his apartment. His life can't get any worse or can it?

Disgraced former CIA agent Andy Flint is brought back by Langley to find out who's killing their agents and changing the balance of power in Russia. Matters become personal for Flint when an old friend is kidnapped. Flint is torn, save his missing friend or get his job back at the agency and rebuild his shattered life.

As Flint's investigation takes him from the corridors of the Kremlin and the frozen streets of Saint Petersburg to the playground of the super-rich in the Caribbean, he discovers the identity of the person from his past who betrayed him. Closing in on the mastermind behind a powerful criminal empire, Flint's life is endangered as he becomes their next target. Can Flint secure the release of his friend, crack the case and deliver justice before his time runs out?

The Makarov File is a stand-alone novel and is first in this series of international thrillers based around CIA agent, Andy Flint.

Dead Secret

Arrested for murder while a ruthless killer is on the loose. Ex-CIA agent Andy Flint uncovers a global conspiracy. Can Flint crack the case before they kill him?

When a United Nations intelligence station in New Zealand is attacked, disgraced former CIA agent Andy Flint is asked to find the sole survivor and uncover why the team were murdered. All the evidence points to his son, Mark as the deadly gunman.

Searching for his son, Flint discovers the CIA are involved. But why? Looking for answers, Flint finds his son is caught up in a deadly conspiracy.

The trail leads Flint from the backstreets of Wellington through the deadly Tararua Mountains to secretive corporate lawyers in Switzerland. With pressure mounting from the CIA, the United Nations and the White House, the real killer is on the loose. Can Flint clear his son's name, find the real murderer and figure out who ordered the murders before the killer zeroes in on him as their next target?

Dead Secret is the second book in the Andy Flint series of international thrillers based around CIA agent, Andy Flint. If you like action, a page turning roller-coaster of a read and plot which keeps you on the edge of your seat, you'll love Peter Kozmar's gripping thriller.

When an innocent coffee almost kills you...

A bomb blows an airliner out of the sky over the Mediterranean killing all on board.

In a hotel in Moscow an Oil Executive wakes up next to a murdered prostitute.

In Brussels, CIA Director Helen Hobbs lies in a coma, clinging by a thread to her life, the victim of a gun attack.

Disgraced former CIA agent Andy Flint is asked by Interpol to find those responsible for shooting Hobbs. As Flint pulls the threads together he becomes the target of a ruthless killer determined to stop him as he uncovers a global conspiracy where the tentacles of corruption spread far and high.

With few he can trust, can Flint solve the mystery and deliver justice before he too finds a place in the morgue?

Zero Trust is the third stand-alone novel in the Andy Flint series of international thrillers based around CIA agent, Andy Flint. If you like action, a page turning roller-coaster of a read and plot which keeps you on the edge of your seat, you'll love Peter Kozmar's gripping thriller

If you'd like to sign up to my newsletter, then please click on the link below and enter your email details. I'll respect your privacy and not share your details with others and you can unsubscribe at any time by emailing me and placing *'Unsubscribe'* in the subject field.

Peter-kozmar.com

Alternatively you can also follow me on social media @peter.kozmar or for those using LinkedIn, look out for Peter Kozmar.

If you enjoyed reading Defector, I'd really appreciate you leaving an honest review about Defector. Reviews help other readers make their decisions on whether the book they are about to read would be right for them. Reviews also help authors improve their visibility within on-line bookstores and your review will help grow my writing career. Success will help me write more and be spurred on to be quicker, which means more of my great stories for you to read.

About the Author

eter was born near Manchester in the North West of England into a working class family. He tudied Engineering at University where he joined the British Army.

During his service he worked in Russia, Ukraine, Belarus, Kazakhstan and Uzbekistan. He spent ignificant time in South Africa before the election of Nelson Mandela. He also spent time briefly in olombia and Mexico. After reaching the rank of Major, he resigned his Commission and moved with is family to New Zealand where he led an active, outdoors life. However, a serious skiing accident neant he wasn't able to run, hike or ski which released a lot of time. That's how the writing started nd allowed him to focus and develop another set of skills

Vith the support of those around him, Peter has written about Andy Flint, starting with The eginning Series. These stories are initially set in 1993 and after the Beginning Series we move orward to find Andy Flint as he is today. A very different man. If you like fast paced, action packed age turners with a thread of conspiracy in your thriller series, then Andy Flint is for you.

eter lives in Wellington, New Zealand. His kids have now left home leaving him with his wife and wo mischievous Labrador's, Brecon and Pembroke.

Made in the USA
Las Vegas, NV
12 January 2023

65511985R00044